THE ROYAL HOUSE OF KAREDES

Large Print Collection

TWO CROWNS, TWO ISLANDS, ONE LEGACY

The islands of Adamas
have been torn into two rival kingdoms
by the royal family's lust for power.
But can passion reunite them?

8 addictive large print volumes

MARCH 2010

Billionaire Prince, Pregnant Mistress
by Sandra Marton

The Sheikh's Virgin Stable-Girl
by Sharon Kendrick

APRIL 2010

The Prince's Captive Wife
by Marion Lennox

The Sheikh's Forbidden Virgin
by Kate Hewitt

MAY 2010

The Greek Billionaire's Innocent Princess
by Chantelle Shaw

The Future King's Love-Child
by Melanie Milburne

JUNE 2010

Ruthless Boss, Royal Mistress
by Natalie Anderson

The Desert King's Housekeeper Bride
by Carol Marinelli

THE SHEIKH'S VIRGIN STABLE-GIRL

Sharon Kendrick

First published in Great Britain 2009
Large Print Edition 2010
Harlequin Mills & Boon Limited,
Eton House, 18-24 Paradise Road, Richmond, Surrey TW9 1SR

© Harlequin Books S.A. 2009

ISBN: 978 0 263 21636 3

THE SHEIKH'S VIRGIN STABLE-GIRL

Special thanks and acknowledgement are given to Sharon Kendrick for her contribution to *The Royal House of Karedes* series.

Harlequin Mills & Boon policy is to use papers that are natural, renewable and recyclable products and made from wood grown in sustainable forests. The logging and manufacturing process conform to the legal environmental regulations of the country of origin.

Printed and bound in Great Britain
by CPI Antony Rowe, Chippenham, Wiltshire

Sharon Kendrick has been writing stories for as long as she can remember and completed her first book at the age of eleven! It featured identical twins fighting evil at their boarding school, but sadly this early manuscript has been lost!

Since then Sharon has gone on to write many books for Mills & Boon and they have been published worldwide. She adores writing romance and considers herself lucky to have the best job in the world! It is a fantastic way to spend a day—inventing gorgeous heroes and complex, interesting women and charting all the ups and downs, the highs and lows of their relationship, until they are really ready to let love into their hearts.

With special thanks to Charlie Brooks,
Andrew Franklin and Jenny Hindmarsh
for making me understand why people
are so passionate about horses.

And to Gerald O'Rourke
for his advice on gambling.

CHAPTER ONE

THERE was no reason why a scorpion shouldn't be lying dead on the ground—but not when Eleni had only just swept the yard. She stared down at its curved black shape and a certainty which defied logic whispered its way in a cold chill over her skin. It was an omen, surely. An evil portent—coming moments before her father's mysterious guest arrived. She swallowed. For wasn't desert legend full of signs as ominous as this?

'Eleni!'

Her father's shout echoed through the hot, still air and Eleni tensed as she tried to work out what kind of mood he was in. At least the tone was steady, which meant that he was sober, but it was impatient, too and her heart sank—for that could mean only one thing. That he was eager to begin his game of cards—and that his fellow players were growing impatient. Loud, laughing men who were stupid enough to gamble away everything they had worked for.

'*Eleni!*' The voice had now become a roar. 'Where in the desert's name are you?'

'I am here, Papa!' she said, quickly kicking the scorpion to a dusty grave in a small pile of sand outside the stables and then hurrying towards the house, where Gamal Lakis stood waiting in the doorway. His wizened and sunburnt face was sour as he looked her up and down.

'What are you doing that keeps you away from the house and your duties?' he criticised.

It was pointless telling him that she had just come from the stables, where she had been speaking softly to his beloved horses. And that such constant care and vigilance kept them in prized and peak condition—making

Gamal Lakis one of the most envied men in this desert kingdom. She knew from experience that there was no explanation that would ever satisfy this most discontented of men.

'I'm sorry, Papa,' she said automatically, lowering her gaze to the ground before looking up once more to flash him a reassuring smile. 'I will come and bring refreshment to your guests immediately.'

'No, no. We cannot yet drink, nor eat the food which has been prepared,' said her father unexpectedly. 'For we await the arrival of our guest of honour.' His faded eyes glinted and he gave a rare and crafty smile. 'And do you know who this guest is, Eleni?'

She shook her head. The visit had been shrouded in mystery for days now, but Eleni knew that it was not her place to ask. Women were told when men deemed that the time was right and not before, especially in households like theirs. 'No, Papa, I do not know.'

'No less than one of the most important men

in the whole of Calista!' he boasted. 'I wonder if you would like to make a guess just who that might be?'

Eleni took her cue, asking him the question he clearly wished to be asked, though his wild extravagance was now making her wonder whether her father was quite as sober as she had first thought.

'Won't you tell me who he is, Papa—so that I may wait on him with due deference when he arrives at our home?'

Gamal's thin lips gave another wet and triumphant smile, pausing like a man who held the trump card in a high-bidding game. 'What would you say, my daughter—if I told you that a royal prince was coming to the home of your father?'

She would say that he *had* been drinking, after all. But never to his face, of course. If Papa was having one of his frequent flights of fancy then it was always best to play along with it.

Eleni kept her face poker-straight. 'A royal prince, Papa?' she questioned gravely.

'Yes, indeed!' He pushed his face forward. 'The Prince Kaliq Al'Farisi,' he crowed, 'is coming to my house to play cards with me!'

Her father had gone insane! These were ideas of grandeur run riot! And what was Eleni to do? What if he continued to make such idle boasts in front of the men who were sitting, waiting to begin the long night of card-playing? Surely that would make him a laughing stock and ruin what little reputation he had left.

'Papa,' she whispered urgently. 'I beg you to think clearly. What place would a royal prince have *here*?'

But she was destined never to hear a reply, even though his mouth had opened like a puppet—for there came the sound of distant hooves. The steady, powerful thud of horses as they thundered over the parched sands. On the still, thick air the muffled beat grew closer and louder until it filled Eleni's ears like the sound of the desert wolves which howled at the silver moon when it was at its fullest.

Towards them galloped a clutch of four horses, and as Eleni watched, one of them broke free and surged forwards like a black stream of oil gushing out of the arid sand. For a moment, she stood there, transfixed—for this was as beautiful and as reckless a piece of riding as she had ever witnessed.

Illuminated by the orange gold of the dying sun, a colossus of a man could be seen, with an ebony stallion between his thighs as he urged it on with a joyful shout. The man's bare head was as dark as the horse he rode and his skin gleamed like some bright and burnished metal. Robes of pure silk clung to the hard sinews of his body and as he approached Eleni could see a face so forbidding that some deep-rooted fear made her wonder if he had the power to turn to dust all those who stood before him.

And a face so inherently beautiful that it was as if all the desert flowers had bloomed at once.

It was then that Eleni understood the full and daunting truth. Her father's bragging *had* been true for riding towards their humble abode was indeed Prince Kaliq Al'Farisi. Kaliq the daredevil, the lover of women, the playboy, the gambler and irresponsible twin son of Prince Ashraf. The man, it was said, could make women moan with pleasure simply by looking at them.

She had not seen him since she was a young girl in the crowds watching the royal family pass by. Back then, he had been doing his military service and wearing the uniform of the Calistan Navy. And back then he had been an arresting young man—barely in his twenties. But now—a decade and a half on—he was at the most magnificent peak of his manhood, with a raw and beautiful masculinity which seemed to shimmer from his muscular frame.

'By the wolves that howl!' Eleni whimpered, and ran inside the house.

'Highness!' simpered Gamal, and as the Prince's horse entered the battered gates he bent as low as his creaking bones would allow.

Kaliq dismounted with the same speed and grace as he would remove himself from the body of a woman he had just made love to. Jumping to the ground, his riding boots dusty beneath the fine, flowing robes which denoted his high status, he glanced around him, making no attempt to hide the faint curve of his lips as he took in his surroundings.

It was as he had thought—a hovel of a place! Lowly and rough—but a place which promised him something which he hungered for. Indeed, his heart's delight. His gaze flickered over the stable door before returning to the grovelling figure before him.

'Get up, Lakis,' he ordered.

Gamal obeyed, rubbing at his back and wincing slightly. 'May I say how honoured am I to have the most venerable prince partake of my—'

'Cut the smarm,' snapped Kaliq, with the arrogance he had learned at one of the many international schools he had attended. An arrogance which had been necessary to protect him from the greed and ambition of those who craved royal patronage. His eyes glittered as he tempered his curt reply with the silken charm which his sister Yasmine complained could lure the birds from the trees.

'I have not come for your craven admiration, Lakis,' he admonished softly. 'But to play cards with a man—and this I have on good authority—a man who is unbeatable at cards. Are you that man, I wonder?'

Gamal smirked and puffed up his chest. 'It has been said, Highness.'

Kaliq drummed an impatient finger on his riding crop. Was the fool not aware that a commoner should never boast of superiority to a royal prince? Idly, he tossed the crop to one of his bodyguards, who was only now just climbing down from his horse and looking a little shamefaced.

'We shall see how unbeatable you are,' Kaliq said carelessly. 'And I am in the mood for good sport tonight—but first I wish to drink. Do you have nothing to offer to quench the parched throats of these travellers, Lakis— for we have ridden long and ridden hard across the desert from our royal palaces?'

'Oh, forgive me, Highness, forgive me,' stumbled Gamal. 'You will please enter my humble abode and anything you desire shall be brought to you.'

The smoke-filled salon was lit by oil-lamps with a bright, spotlight glare over the poker table and Kaliq dipped his head as he entered the room, noting that one of his bodyguards had slipped in before him. The faint scent of incense mingled with the smell of tobacco and the deep voices grew silent as the assembled men sprang instantly to their feet.

Kaliq's smile was wolfish as he waved at them to resume their seats. For wasn't the number one rule of defeating the opposition to first give them a false sense of security? 'No, no. Tonight you do not stand on ceremony; tonight we are as equals,' he instructed softly. 'For the cards cannot be played properly if one insists on hierarchy. Tonight I am not a prince of your land—I am simply a man, just like you, Lakis.'

Standing just outside the door and summoning up the courage to enter the room, Eleni wondered if her father knew what he was up against. Because as she listened to the prince's drawled statement, it somehow didn't ring quite true. As if this powerful prince would ever desire that these ruffians should be his equal!

'Eleni!'

She was just about to call, 'Yes, Papa,' when she heard his next words.

'My servant girl will bring us food and drink! Eleni—come now!'

In spite of her nerves, Eleni almost smiled. How wily her father was. Not only was he elevating his status in front of the prince by bringing in an extra, female servant—but by using his daughter he would guarantee absolute discretion. As well as not having to pay her anything!

Sucking in a deep breath, Eleni entered the room, keeping her eyes down and resisting the terrible overwhelming instinct which made her long to look at the prince again, which wasn't easy since servants were never permitted eye-contact with a member of the ruling family of Calista. She knew too that protocol demanded she make a deep curtsey—not something she was used to doing.

'Your Highness,' she said softly, and, bending one knee behind the other, she made a sweeping kind of bow—glad that all her years of riding had given her a certain grace. 'What does my master request that I should bring to his honoured guest?' she added quietly.

Kaliq glanced over at her, his antennae automatically alerted by the sound of a woman's voice. It was soft and soothing, he thought—like cool, running water running through this oppressive and stuffy room. And it was curiously fluent for a servant. His eyes narrowed, but he could not see whether she was plain or beautiful.

Her head was covered with a veil and the clothes she wore were drab and concealing— and while they were entirely appropriate for a woman of her class and status, he would have preferred to feast his eyes on something attractive. Some buxom young thing with her breasts half spilling out, who would pleasure him with the yearning in her eyes!

'A drink,' he ordered curtly, forcing his thoughts away from the subject because he was here tonight to play cards—not to lose himself in the delights of a woman.

'You will drink some *Zelyoniy* with us?' questioned Gamal hopefully.

Kaliq suppressed a shudder. As if he could bring himself to drink *Zelyoniy*! The potent green spirit made from cactus plants was banned in most of the country, though he knew that its use was still widespread in the rougher regions. But might it not assist his game if his partners were partial to hard liqueur? 'Not for me,' he answered silkily. 'But the rest of you must drink what pleases you. Bring me pomegranate juice instead,' he told the servant girl.

'At once, Highness,' said Eleni, and hurried off.

Kaliq leaned back in his chair as the dealer opened the new pack of cards and a familiar excitement began to steal over his skin. He wanted to win, yes, because he loved winning—but more important than victory was the risk involved. He shouldn't really be here, associating with these low-life racehorse breeders and trainers—but that, of course, only added to the evening's appeal. The sense of the unknown, the forbidden and the elicit.

Because sometimes Kaliq grew bored with his privileged life—a life which took him to cities all over the Western world. Cities where he could slip easily into the role of the playboy sheikh—as the international newspapers were so fond of calling him. Impossibly rich from the wealth of his country's diamond mines, he could have anything he wanted—and mostly he did.

But sometimes he wanted harsh contrast and that was what brought him to places like this. Where the hardships and toughness of desert life made the fleshpots of Europe fade into insignificance. As the cards began to be dealt around the table Kaliq felt the familiar thrill of expectation.

'You will take food, Highness?'

Kaliq glanced up. The servant girl was standing before him and putting a goblet of pomegranate juice before him. He shook his dark head impatiently. As if he would eat with people such as these!

'No. I have no appetite for food.' And then he glanced at the drink. 'But my thirst is great. Taste it,' he instructed the girl.

Eleni's heart raced in confusion. Surely the prince did not intend her to drink from *his* glass? 'But—'

'I said, taste it,' he repeated softly. 'Or I will begin to worry that you are trying to poison me.'

With nervous fingers Eleni lifted the heavy cup—her father's best—to her lips and sipped at the sweet, tangy juice, the tip of her tongue automatically removing its sticky trace from her lips. How horrible for the prince to have to live with such terrible fears, she thought, her heart giving an automatic little tug of compassion. Did he have to watch his back, wherever he went, she wondered—afraid that some unknown assassin was lurking in the shadows?

Aware that his piercing black eyes were fixed on her, she felt as if she had been turned to stone. What was she supposed to do now?

And how long did they have to wait to see if she had been poisoned?

'Well?' Kaliq shot the word out.

Eleni swallowed as she stared down at the goblet. 'I think the drink will please you, Highness.'

'Then give it to me,' he ordered silkily.

At this, she was forced to lift her gaze upwards as she held the juice towards him and as Kaliq stared into her face he felt the first shimmering of astonishment. For she had green eyes—pale green and glittering! The fabled green eyes of Calista—a throwback to warriors from Persia who had briefly conquered this land and its women many centuries ago, before being defeated by one of his ancestors. Legendary eyes—rare and lovely and spoken of in the palaces and tea rooms—but he had never seen them before now.

'By the desert storm,' he murmured beneath his breath, a strange wild beating in his heart as he sipped some of the juice and stared into them. 'Such beautiful eyes.'

But then the cards began to fly from the dealer's hands and Kaliq turned his attention to the game, the servant dismissed from his mind, her eyes forgotten.

There was a lot of money at stake, but it soon became clear to Kaliq that he and Gamal were playing to a different agenda from the other men, and soon their natural aggression ensured that there were only two of them left in the game. But Gamal was drinking too much alcohol—and Kaliq knew that there was one place in the world where you could not afford to be drunk, and that was at the poker table.

As the dealer skimmed them each two cards he saw Gamal try and fail to hide his smile of triumph and Kaliq sensed that his moment was drawing near. He looked up to find that the green eyes of the servant girl were fixed on the table with a look of terror. Was she perhaps worried that her master would gamble away all his livelihood, and her job into the bargain?

Glancing down at his own cards, Kaliq leaned forward. 'A thousand to play,' he said softly to the soft gasp of one of the onlookers.

Gamal immediately pushed a pile of *hyakim* notes into the pot. 'Three thousand,' he croaked, licking his lips.

Kaliq leaned back in his chair, sensing the man's greed and certainty that he was going to win and the prince smiled with the confidence of a man who held an unbeatable pair of cards in his hand. 'You look as if you'd like to bet more, Lakis,' he said silkily. 'Shall we raise the stakes? I'll allow you to make a larger bet if you wish.'

Gamal's eyes gleamed. 'How much?'

Kaliq shrugged. 'Well, as you know, I have no use for money—but if you want to sweeten the pot with that Arab stallion of yours that I've heard so much about, then I'll put in a million. What do you say to that, old man?'

Unable to believe what she was seeing, Eleni dropped a spoon in an attempt to bring her father to his senses but the atmosphere in the room was so tense that nobody even noticed it clattering to the ground. This was like a bad, bad dream—her drunken brute of a father threatening to use his prize stallion as a wager. Her own beloved horse and just about the only thing which kept her sane in the harsh environment in which she lived.

'A million, you say?' questioned Gamal greedily.

'A million,' agreed Kaliq.

Eleni wanted to scream at her father not to persist with this foolishness—for even she could see from the prince's demeanour that he *must* hold the winning cards. But how could she possibly boldly assert herself in this company of men, and in front of their royal guest? Why, Kaliq would probably have one of his bodyguards carry her from the room and slapped into the jailhouse in Serapolis!

'Would…would you care for another drink, Highness?' she questioned desperately, hoping to shatter the mood with her inappropriate question.

'Do not dare speak to me when we are engaged in play,' snapped Kaliq.

'Yes, yes. I'll wager the stallion!' butted in Gamal wildly, triumphantly slapping two kings down on the table.

Eleni bunched her fist into her mouth. 'No!' she whimpered, but nobody heard. She could hardly bear to watch, but it was as inevitable as watching the sun sink down over the distant mountains. Her father was going to lose, or rather, the prince was going to win—that much had been apparent from the moment he had first galloped up on his own magnificent stallion.

Slowly, Kaliq laid down his two aces—the only hand which could beat Gamal's—and there was a collective gasp in the room. 'My game, I think,' he said softly.

Eleni honestly thought that she might faint,

and on shaky knees she staggered to the door, not caring if it was discourteous to their royal guest to leave without being dismissed, not caring about anything—because to all intents and purposes her life was over.

She took one last look at Kaliq's beautiful hard face and the cruel smile which curved his lips—and her fingers itched to pick up the heavy spoon she had dropped and to hurl it at his arrogant royal head. How dared he try to rob them of the one thing in their lives which brought them income and prosperity?

Half stumbling out into the now-dark night, Eleni ran to the stable block before letting herself into the stall of her beloved Nabat, who whinnied with pleased recognition when he saw her and came nuzzling around her hand for a piece of sugar.

'Oh, Nabat,' she whispered as she put her arms around his sleek neck and buried her face in his sweet-smelling fur. 'Darling, darling Nabat—how will I ever be able to cope without you?' She pulled her face back to look deep into the horse's face, seeming to see bewilderment written in the creature's eyes. Or was she doing that age-old thing of animal lovers and transferring *her* feelings onto Nabat?

This was the horse who had arrived as a long-legged young foal and even then she had seen the beauty, strength and potential inherent in the animal. But it had been an unhappy horse. She didn't know how her father had managed to acquire the fine Arabian stallion and she hadn't wanted to know—all she *did* know was that it had been badly in need of some tender loving care.

In those early days when Nabat had been fretful and rearing and baring his teeth whenever anyone went near him, it had been Eleni who had soothed him, who had taken the time to coax him to eat.

'The animal is too highly strung!' Gamal had complained on more than one occasion, his hand straying towards the large whip he loved to carry. 'Maybe we should beat some manners into it!'

But Eleni had sprung to the helpless creature's defence. 'No, Papa!' she had pleaded. 'Let me try to school him for you, to settle him down so that he's happy here.'

'He had better be happy soon enough!' her father had snarled. 'Or he will find himself for sale on a kebab stand in Aquila!'

So by nights Eleni had slept in the straw at the other end of the stable—like a mother attending to a fretful newborn—and in the end she and her father had both been rewarded. For her had come the kind of unconditional love she had never been shown by a human since her mother had died. And for her father—well, he began to revel in the riches which came as a result of the horse blossoming into a soon-legendary winner of every race he was entered into.

Was that why the prince wanted him? To

reap some of Nabat's athletic glory onto his worthless and spoilt royal head?

Her arms tightened around the Arab's neck. 'Well, I will not leave you, Nabat,' she said fiercely. 'That I promise you. I'll stow away in the very straw that transports you away from me. And when I get the opportunity, we will escape together—to find a life of peace and quiet.'

She wondered when the sheikh would come to claim his spoils. Presumably, he would need time to arrange for Nabat to be taken to the royal palace. Which gave her time to arrange how best to hide herself and the few meagre belongings she would need to take with her.

But at that moment she heard the sound of men talking—and in particular the arrogant and autocratic drawl of the sheikh's voice carrying across the yard. *And it was heading this way*!

Her heart racing, she sprang away from the horse's neck but it was too late—for the soft light of an oil-lamp spilled its light across the stable, illuminating her in its golden glow.

She could see little of the man holding the lamp—save for the hard glitter of his eyes and the pale shimmer of his silken robes—and Eleni stood there, frozen with all kinds of conflicting emotions, feeling as guilty as if she had been found in the arms of a lover.

'*You,*' said Kaliq damningly as his eyes swept over her. 'What in the falcon's name are you doing here?'

CHAPTER TWO

HER fears banished by the harsh reality of what was about to happen, Eleni stared at the sheikh with sheer hatred in her eyes—choking out the words as if they were sour berries.

'I was just…just saying goodbye to my horse.'

'*Your* horse?' He stepped closer. 'I think you forget yourself in more ways than one, girl. This is the horse I have just won from your master in a card game—and do you not curtsey when your sheikh appears before you?'

Her hurt was such that Eleni was tempted to defy him—to tell him that she would rather curtsey to a camel than curtsey to him—but what would that achieve? Because—as her father himself had boasted before he had been taken for a fool—Prince Kaliq Al'Farisi was one of the most powerful men in the whole of Calista. Why tempt the fury of a man like that?

'Highness,' she murmured as she sank briefly downwards.

Kaliq ran his eyes over her. There was something in her attitude which perplexed him. Something which did not quite add up. Why was a mere female servant bothered about what happened to her master's horse?

'Explain yourself!' he commanded.

His voice cracked out like a whip and instinctively Eleni flinched. He was no different from her cruel father, she thought bitterly. No different from all men with their harsh and domineering ways. Did he really expect her to speak freely to him? He, who was a man *and* a stranger *and* a royal prince—especially when one of his bodyguards was hovering in the background?

'What is it that you wish me to explain, Highness?' Eleni questioned woodenly.

Kaliq had seen those huge eyes darting over at his bodyguard. And he remembered their alluring colour, too... As bewitching a colour as he had ever seen. 'Be gone,' he said, dismissing his bodyguard peremptorily.

'But, Highness—'

Kaliq turned to the burly minder, a look of contempt curving his lips. 'You think that I need your protection against this tiny lizard of a girl?' he questioned, elevating his black brows in arrogant query. 'Or perhaps you think that she needs mine?'

'*No*, Highness!'

'Quite right—for a sheikh does not concern himself with scruffy little urchins like this! So be gone,' Kaliq repeated, with an edge of anger to his voice, and the man slipped out of the stables.

Eleni stood there, waiting for the interrogation to begin, but the sheikh was nothing if not unpredictable. Completely ignoring her, he walked over to study the horse, running his experienced eyes over the animal's gleaming flesh and lithe limbs. Kaliq gave a slow smile of satisfaction. Up close the creature was even more magnificent than when he had seen it from a distance on the racetrack last week.

He took a step forwards but Nabat gave a nervous whinny and jerked back into the corner. Anxiously, Eleni watched and waited to see whether the prince would show the same dominance and aggression as he had exhibited at the poker table, but to her surprise he did not. Instead, he turned around and subjected her to a long, slow scrutiny which suddenly made her feel very peculiar indeed. No man had ever looked at her in such a way before. *And no man should*, she thought weakly, wondering what had caused her heart to pound so distractingly, or her skin to tingle and glow.

'Stroke the horse,' he instructed.

'But—'

'Do *not* question me,' he cut in icily. '*Never*

question the sheikh—did they not teach you that in school, girl?'

Of course they did. Basic instruction in protocol was part of the Calistan history course and taught in every village school in the country. And these days even lowly servants went to school—by order of Queen Anya, who had overhauled the outdated system and insisted that every child in the land should have the opportunity to acquire a rudimentary education.

But, unsurprisingly, Eleni's history lessons had not included a section on how a lowly commoner should behave when she was alone in a stable with a sheikh! And not just any sheikh, either—but the arrogant playboy who was about to take from her the only thing in the world which she had ever truly loved.

'Forgive me, Highness,' she said unconvincingly.

Kaliq's eyes glinted. In his thirty-six years he had heard enough variations on deference to know that such respect was distinctly lacking in this girl's attitude. In fact, her whole manner simmered with a kind of suppressed anger. How dared she? And what lay behind such intolerable insolence?

'Stroke the horse,' he repeated silkily.

This time she could not refuse him. Eleni approached Nabat, who immediately came trotting out from the corner, making little snorting sounds of delight as he began to nuzzle at her hand for sugar. And the warmth of his dear breath on her fingers was enough to dispel Eleni's nerves and for her to momentarily forget where she was, and with whom.

'No, no, my sweet!' she laughed. 'I have no treat for you today!' She heard the intake of the sheikh's breath and she looked up to find him watching her as a snake might fix its eyes on the charmer.

'Who are you?' he questioned slowly.

'My name…is Eleni.'

He shook his head impatiently. 'Your name

is of no interest to me.' Staring deep into her distractingly beautiful eyes, he lowered his voice. 'I want to know why you are so familiar with a creature of such value as this.'

'Because…' Eleni bit her lip. She could see the hard and forbidding lines of his face and her heart sank. What a fool she was. Did she really think that she would have been able to stow away and be smuggled into the royal stables in order to be near her beloved horse? Couldn't she imagine how formidable this man's anger would be when he discovered her, as discover her he inevitably would?

No. So could she not risk telling him the truth?

'Because I have cared for this horse since he first came to these stables!' she declared. 'When Nabat was little more than a badly treated young foal!'

'Nabat?'

'The stallion's name. It means sweetness—like the pieces of yellow sugar you crush between your fingers on market day. He answers to that,' she added stubbornly.

'Go on,' said Kaliq in an odd kind of voice.

'I washed and brushed him and coaxed him to take food from my hand. It was I who first mounted him bareback,' she said, a strange warmth glowing in her heart as she remembered that glorious day when she had ridden him around the yard. 'And I who first put the saddle on his back.' Eleni swallowed. 'At first he did not like it—this is a breed of horse who instinctively wishes to be free. But, gradually, he allowed himself to become comfortable with it. And I...I—'

At this, her voice broke as she tried to imagine a world without Nabat and suddenly all restraint left her as she forgot the rank of the dark-eyed man who stood before her. 'I love this creature,' she whispered, and her heart ached so much that she completely disregarded the first tear which slid slowly down her cheek.

But Kaliq stared at her incredulously. A servant daring to show emotion in front of her sheikh! How dared she? 'Dry your eyes,' he ordered harshly, steeling his heart to the sparkle of tears which made her eyes look so huge and so brilliantly green. 'And then answer my question as I wish it to be answered!'

'But I just have,' objected Eleni as she swiftly wiped the rogue tears away.

'No,' he said witheringly. 'You have not. You have failed to satisfy my curiosity to know why you, a poor and humble servant girl who waits on the table of drunken gamblers, should be given access to care for such a valuable commodity.'

She wanted to tell him that Nabat was not a *commodity* but she sensed that such an indulgence would add fuel to an anger which was already growing more ominous by the minute. He wanted the truth, did he? Then very well— she would give it to him in pure and unvarnished form.

'Because I am not a *poor and humble servant girl*, Your Highness.' Eleni sucked in a deep breath. 'I am actually the daughter of your host, Gamal.'

His *daughter*? Kaliq's jaw tightened with disbelief. 'So what was that charade I have just witnessed in there with you waiting on me?' he demanded, his eyes searing over her with scorn. 'And did you dress dowdily to make yourself look like a servant?'

Eleni said nothing for she would rather die than admit these were her normal clothes.

'Did you beg your father for the privilege of waiting on one such as your sheikh?' he queried arrogantly. 'Did you wish to feast your eyes on a true man for once?'

Never in all her days had Eleni heard such an outrageous example of self-love. And no matter what his position in society—he had no right to cast doubts on her integrity and her purity as a woman.

'No, Highness, I did not,' she replied, staring

angrily at the ground. 'For such behaviour would not be fitting.'

'Then why?'

'Because—'

'Look at me!' he demanded. 'When you speak to me.'

Slowly, she lifted her eyes, feeling as if she were struggling to free herself from a heavy weight which had been pressing down on her—for how could you suddenly abandon a lifetime's teaching in one instant? To abandon the demureness which was drummed into every female and to stare into the face of one of the mightiest and most daunting in the land. But what choice did she have? 'As you wish, Your Highness,' she said reluctantly.

Kaliq found himself sucking in a deep breath as she obeyed him. He would never normally have told a woman to look at him and particularly not a woman such as this, but wasn't there some inexplicable and insistent yearning to grant himself one more look at those incredible eyes? Like a man who had been given a fleeting glimpse of paradise and wanted reassurance that he had not simply imagined it…

He expelled the breath from a throat which suddenly felt dry and scorched as the light from the lamp illuminated the glittering eyes. They were the most remarkable hue he had ever seen—pale green as the strange colour which streaked the arctic skies and which were called the Northern Lights.

'Explain to me your motives for pretending to be Gamal's servant instead of his daughter,' he said, and for a moment his voice was almost kind.

There was a pause. Their lives were so different—would he understand, even if she attempted to explain? 'We do not keep many servants,' admitted Eleni shamefacedly—for was not a family's worth assessed by the volume of staff they employed?

'Oh? And why is that?'

Was he deliberately wishing to make her squirm? Couldn't he work out the reason for himself without her having to draw the words on the sand for him? What a cruel and arrogant man he was. 'It is a question of finance, Highness,' she said proudly.

'Is it now?' Kaliq wondered softly as he looked around him. Although in need of work and renovation, the stables were a good size, as was the living accommodation. He suspected that there had once been money enough for servants, but that Gamal had drunk and gambled most of it away.

He moved a step closer towards her and Eleni was suddenly aware of the raw and potent aura of his masculinity and her heart began to thunder with fear, and with something else, too—something terrifying and unrecognisable.

'So what are you doing here?' he questioned. 'Why did I find you with your arms around my horse, and looking so guilty?'

It almost broke Eleni's heart to hear that

drawled and possessive question. *My* horse, he had said—and he spoke nothing but the truth. For Nabat *was* his horse—given up as a prize in a common game of poker! And soon he would be gone to a life of luxury in one of the royal stables and she would never see him again. Couldn't he—even if he had a lump of stone for a heart—guess how much she was hurting at the thought of having to say goodbye to the only thing in the world that she loved?

The words burst out of her mouth as if she had no control over them. 'I could not bear the thought of being without my…your horse,' she corrected painfully. 'And so I concocted a plan to ensure that I wouldn't need to be.'

At this, Kaliq's lips curved into an indulgent smile. 'Oh? And do you want to tell me what your plan is, little lizard?'

She hated his sardonic tone, the mocking expression in those dark and glittering eyes, and she hated the way he had looked her up and down, as if she were some invisible lump of rags.

'I was going to hide myself away—so that when you came to take him away, you would have to take me, as well,' she told him, her brittle words daring him to taunt her, but to her surprise he did not—merely narrowed his eyes in thought as if she had said something entirely unexpected.

'You do not think that you would have been discovered? That one of the palace guards would not have found you out and driven a sword through your heart, thinking that you might be about to make an assassination attempt on my life?'

She remembered him making her taste his juice in case it was poisoned and once again Eleni thought that, for all his wealth and power and status, his must be a very lonely and frightening position to be in sometimes.

'I was not thinking of myself,' she answered.

'No. I can see that.' He raised his hand to rake

his fingers through his thick black hair and once again the horse gave a nervous whinny.

'He doesn't like men,' said Eleni helpfully.

'He will soon learn to like them.'

Eleni thought that he meant to use the whip, as her father had threatened to do so often. 'And he doesn't respond well to harsh treatment, either!' she defended.

For a moment, Kaliq almost smiled. Standing there in her plain and dowdy clothes—barely higher than his chest—she nonetheless made him admire her courage. Few would have spoken to him with such candour and such passion unless it concerned wealth or ambition.

'Horses are like women,' he said softly. 'And neither respond well to harsh treatment.'

And to Eleni's horror she began to blush—from where her veil touched her scalp, all the way down to the tips of her toes. Not that blushing was a crime and nor was there anything in the protocol books which suggested that it might be discourteous, but to blush as a result of such a statement made it look…look…*as if she were imagining how she would respond to the sheikh as a woman*! And wasn't she? *Wasn't* she?

Now Kaliq did smile. 'Do not worry, little lizard,' he drawled. 'You will be perfectly safe with me.'

The meaning behind his words was abundantly clear—even to someone of Eleni's inexperience of the ways of men. Of course she—a humble girl from the country—would be safe from the attentions of the powerful and experienced sheikh. She would not have expected anything else. Yet stupidly and unexpectedly, it hurt—that he should be so openly dismissive of her. As if he would sooner cavort with one of the desert ravens than entertain the thought of being with a scruffy servant girl.

But Eleni forced herself to put such idle musings out of her mind. She suspected that he was mulling something over in his mind—something to do with Nabat, and perhaps to do with her, too. And something which she had thought had died many years ago began to flicker into life.

Hope.

Instinct told her to remain silent—as if her words might shatter possibility as she waited for the sheikh to speak.

'You have nurtured the horse,' observed Kaliq slowly.

'Yes, Highness.'

'He knows you and responds well to you.'

'Yes, Highness.'

'And how do you think he'll behave without you?'

She was tempted to embellish and paint a dramatic picture of how Nabat would play up without his mistress—but Eleni realised that she didn't have to do anything except speak the truth.

'He will hate it, Highness.'

'He will go off his food, you mean? Pine?'

'Yes, Highness.'

'Like a lovesick fool?' he scorned.

Briefly, her eyelids shuttered her eyes before she remembered his command and lifted her gaze to his face. 'I wouldn't know about that, Highness.'

'You think perhaps that he will die without you, little lizard?'

She wished he wouldn't call her that—just as she wished that she could make herself sound completely indispensable. But that would be a lie and she guessed he would see right through it.

'No, Highness,' she said softly. 'I do not, for the desire to live overpowers everything—indeed, it is the strongest force in all the world.' She wondered why his hard face had suddenly tightened into a harsh mask and she rushed on, afraid that she had somehow angered him but still determined to state her case. 'The horse will not die but he will be miserable without me, and a miserable horse does not win races.'

He nodded. 'So what do you suggest as a solution for this particular problem?'

It was strange how fear could give you courage. Or maybe not so strange at all when you considered that Nabat was her only friend in the world. 'The only solution you have, Highness,' she said boldly. 'You take me with you.'

It would have been almost funny if it had not been so preposterous. '*You*? A tiny upstart of a girl? Why, your mother would never forgive me.'

There was a pause. Her gaze flew to a zigzag of hay which lay on the stable floor and she stared at it with fierce concentration. 'But I have no mother, Highness.'

At this, Kaliq stilled—for was there not a more brutal and defining bond than the loss of a mother? He had been just nine when his own mother had died giving birth to his brother

Zafir, and that first and terrible loss had seemed to bring tragedy in its wake for Kaliq and his twin brother. His mouth hardened.

'What happened?' he questioned softly.

Eleni shrugged her shoulders as if she was trying to shrug away the intrusive question. It was funny—you could tell yourself that you had come to terms with something which had happened years ago, but still that rogue little edge of abandonment could make your heart catch with pain. 'My mother died,' she said woodenly.

Kaliq's eyes narrowed. 'Died of what—a desert fever?'

'I don't believe so, Highness.'

'Then what?'

Eleni hesitated. He was very persistent—but when had anyone last shown this kind of interest in her? Come to think of it—when had anyone last bothered to mention her green-eyed mother who had found it so difficult to adapt to married life? Her father certainly never did—he had obliterated her from his memory, and, even if he hadn't exactly banned the use of her name in the Gamal house, Eleni didn't dare to speak it for fear of his reaction.

'My father was displeased with his dinner,' Eleni began, vaguely recalling the noise and the drunken shouts and the mess of lentils splattered all over the floor. 'He sent my mother to market to buy a chicken and on the way back she stumbled, and fell.' Eleni swallowed. 'They think that she was bitten by a snake—but by the time they found her, she was dead and the vultures had long taken away the chicken.'

By the muscular shafts of his thighs, Kaliq's hands clenched into two tight fists. He had been accused by women of having not a shred of compassion in his hard body but for once he found himself touched by this urchin's plight. 'And how old were you?' he demanded.

'I was…ten.'

Ten? Almost the same age as *he* had been when his mother died in childbirth. Kaliq turned away from her troubled and trembling face, unwilling to acknowledge another fierce spear of recognition which burned through him—because some things were better buried away, deep in the dark recesses of memory. Royal and commoner—united by a strange bond. Each and every one of them had their burdens, he recognised bitterly—it was just that some were darker than others. With an efficiency born out of years of practice, he pushed his thoughts away.

Logic told him to dismiss this motherless little stable girl with a curse in her ear for her presumptuousness. As if *she* would have any place in his stables!

And yet undoubtedly she spoke the truth about the horse. Would he not perform better if she were taken along, too? Would not it be infinitely more preferable to spare his stable staff the trouble of having to break in a highly strung horse who might still sulk and refuse to race properly?

He turned back—seeing that this time she had not dropped her gaze, but was meeting his with a steady question in her eyes. The little lizard grew brave for the love of her horse! 'Your father will miss you,' he commented.

'Yes, Highness.'

He observed her involuntary wince at an observation he suspected was untrue, but noted that she did not blacken the man's name. So she was loyal, too. That was good. In fact, it was a quality he required above all others. He guessed that her drunken oaf of a father was unkind and worthless, but he also suspected that there would be no real role for the girl now that his most precious asset had been gambled away. And what would she do in the horse's absence? Continue to care and to wait on him and his useless friends until her youth had fled and she was a wizened old crone?

'You wish to come with me? As my stable girl?'

Eleni stared at him, scarcely able to believe what he was saying. Her heart was beating so loud that it seemed to fill the stable. 'Oh, yes, please, Highness,' she whispered urgently, and dropped her gaze to the ground once more, 'Please, yes!'

'Then I want you to look at me at all times when I'm talking to you,' he told her harshly.

'But…'

'If you're going to be working for me, then you will be treated just the same as the stable boys. Sometimes if a horse is troubled then it is necessary to communicate silently— through eye-contact. And in any case, I don't like having a conversation with the top of someone's head—is that understood?'

'Yes, Highness.'

Kaliq's mind began to skate over the practicalities of such a step. Would such a decision to bring a woman back with him excite comment in the fevered courtrooms of the royal palaces? Very probably—but didn't he thrive on his maverick reputation? He gave a brief, hard smile as he called out for his body-guard, who slipped into the stable with the stealth and speed of dark light. 'We are taking this girl with us,' Kaliq said.

The man's face remained impassive. 'We are, Highness?'

'She is to be my stable girl—with sole re-sponsibility for the new stallion. Arrange a price with her father,' ordered Kaliq. 'Whatever you think she is worth. And then bring her to my royal palace.'

He swept from the stable in a shimmer of silken robes, without another glance or word in her direction, and once again Eleni bit her lip—this time to keep the useless shimmer of tears away from the hostile glance of his bodyguard.

Because, yes, in a way—the royal sheikh had come to her rescue. She would not need to be parted from her beloved Nabat after all, and she would be free of this dark and dingy world in which she had existed ever since her mother had died.

But let it never be forgotten that Prince Kaliq Al'Farisi had just ordered his body-guard to buy her—as if she were a sack of chickpeas on sale at Serapolis market!

CHAPTER THREE

'BY THE desert's storm!' murmured Eleni with a sense of wonder as she gently drew the horse to a halt. Her arduous journey over the inhospitable desert terrain was forgotten as she gazed up at Prince Kaliq's magnificent palace—easily visible from the magnificent stable block where she had been taken and which was to be her new home.

She still couldn't quite believe she was here—that her father had let her go so easily. He had simply shrugged his shoulders when she'd gone to say goodbye.

'You are just like your mother.' He had scowled. 'I shan't miss you.' Then he had spat a piece of tobacco onto the ground and Eleni had shuddered. She suspected that he would miss her more than he anticipated—and wondered how he would feel about having to pay someone to cater to his every whim. The sheikh must have given him a princely sum, Eleni realised—for her father to accept her leaving the family home without trying to give her a beating.

And now she had a new home. A sheikh's palace—surrounded by gardens of unbelievable splendour which seemed to make a mockery of the harsh desert which lay outside its high walls. Again, Eleni shook her head in wonder.

'It's so beautiful,' she blurted out.

'Indeed, it is famed for its loveliness,' agreed the bodyguard, who had accompanied her on the long ride from her father's home. 'Sometimes the people arrive at the gate to pay homage to His Highness—they leave flowers for him and sweetmeats, too. And naturally the women come—to gaze upon his face.' He turned to Eleni. 'You have never seen the prince's home before?'

'No, never,' Eleni said shyly as she dismounted Nabat and stroked his gleaming flank.

She had seen the main Calistan palace of course—in its strategic position which overlooked the busy Port of Aquila. She remembered her mother taking her there once on Flag Day—which was Calista's biggest national holiday.

And what a bright and colourful day it had been—just the two of them—and the last such trip before her mother's death. Maybe that was why it was etched for ever in Eleni's memory.

The streets had been bursting with throngs of people who had flocked from all over Calista—all waving their flags and eager to see the royal procession as it passed through. To a young girl who was a stranger to the city, Eleni had been excited for days beforehand.

She had worn her best tunic with the matching trousers which Calistan women of all ages wore, and her long, thick hair had been woven with a pale green ribbon the same colour as her eyes. Beneath the wide, shady canopy of the date-trees which lined the route, her mother had given her sugared almonds and dried melon to eat. They had drunk the sweet juice of pomegranates while one of the court performers had sung the *Destan*, which was an epic poem sung in honour of the royal family.

As the coaches had gone by, Eleni remembered thinking how serene Queen Anya looked—and what a wonderful woman she must have been to have taken on Sheikh Ashraf's seven motherless children. Seven! Imagine that. And she remembered her eyes being drawn to the ruggedly handsome Kaliq and wondering why his twin brother Aarif was nowhere to be seen.

Now she stared at the blue and golden palace which glittered in the afternoon sun with a faint sense of disbelief clinging to her skin. Who would ever have thought that she—Eleni

Lakis—would one day stand in front of that same Kaliq's home, employed as his stable girl! That his home was to be her home?

'You will be shown to your quarters,' said the bodyguard, but Eleni shook her head.

'Thank you, but that must come later. First, I must settle Nabat into his new home.'

'One of the lads will do that for you.'

'No.' Eleni shook her head firmly. She was aware of her responsibilities and aware too of how important it was for her to remain valuable to the sheikh. Because what would happen if she displeased him? Might he not send her packing straight back to her father?

She shuddered. Surely he would not do that. Hadn't she sensed that the sheikh understood her relief to be away from the repressive and limited future which had lain ahead of her— or was that just wishful thinking on her part? No matter. She must now show him that he had made a wise decision to bring her here with him. She would be loyal. She would work her fingers to the bone. Up at first light and last to bed—she would make herself so indispensable that the sheikh would wonder how he had ever managed to run a successful stable without her!

'I must do it myself,' she said stubbornly.

The bodyguard shrugged. 'Then I will return in half an hour with a female servant who will show you to your quarters.'

But Eleni barely noticed him go as her eyes drank in the royal stable complex. Here was everything a horse could possibly want—comfort, space and security—and for the first time she appreciated what a wonderful time Nabat was going to have.

Hosing him down until he was good and wet, she scraped him off, then gave him some hay and a drink. She was just putting a rug on his back when she heard the sound of footfall behind her and some instinct made her turn round and a strange shiver whispered its way over her skin when she saw just who stood there.

It was Kaliq.

He was standing in the doorway, the illumination of the magnificent sky behind him throwing his tall figure into silhouette. But the dark outline only seemed to emphasise his muscular physique and dominating presence—as vibrant and as powerful as the stallion itself.

A strange tremble began to whisper its way over her skin and her heart began to pound in that way which made Eleni feel very slightly faint. She wanted to seek sanctity from that blazing black gaze by looking at the ground as she had been taught over a lifetime of lessons in modesty and subservience. Yet had not the sheikh himself forbidden her to do that?

Ignoring the girl completely, Kaliq stood staring at the horse, just admiring the sheer magnificence of his latest acquisition until something untoward caught his eye. His lips curving with distaste, he walked over to the horse and lifted a corner of the worn rug which lay over the animal's back. 'What is *this*?' he questioned acidly.

'A rug, Highness,' said Eleni helpfully. 'I brought it with me. I always cover Nabat's back with straw after I've hosed him down and then put this rug straight on top—you can see I have punched holes in it, so that the excess water can escape during the night. It is an excellent method of keeping the horse comfortable and dry.'

Kaliq was now staring at her in disbelief. 'You mean, that you've brought this filthy old blanket with you all the way from your father's house?' he demanded.

She willed herself not to react to the insult. 'Yes, Highness.'

'But what about your clothes? Your belongings?'

'They're in that holdall over there,' she said, pointing.

He scowled at the modestly sized and

threadbare carpet-bag which was sitting on the straw. 'And that's *all* you've brought?'

'Yes.' Shamefully, Eleni felt a blush begin to stain her cheeks.

'But you're supposed to be here for good!' he exploded. 'Not for an overnight stay!'

'There is no problem—I can wash my clothes out by hand every night, Highness. It is what I am used to.'

The irony did not escape him. One moment she was modestly looking at the ground—and yet now she was telling her prince about washing out her most intimate garments! Kaliq felt a slow rage begin to simmer in his blood—and not simply because she had been insubordinate. No, because that flush of pink to her cheeks had made her eyes look as green as pistachios and as bright as new leaves— and, unwittingly and inappropriately, he could feel the sudden hot stir of lust at his groin.

It was a familiar ache. An appetite which demanded to be fed. Desire could sometimes be all the more powerful when it was indiscriminate—and Kaliq was a highly sexed man.

Part of him wanted to throw her down onto the straw and have done with it. For there was no surer way of losing desire for a woman than to take your fill of her. But he sensed that Eleni might be slow to realise that her duty was to please her sheikh in every aspect that he demanded. His mouth curved into a smile. She would soon learn.

'You may be a stable girl with nothing in the way of social engagements—but you are also a representative of the royal house of Al'Farisi,' he bit out as he forced his mind away from the hard ache at his groin. 'And as such—you will not be dressed in rags and looking like a scullery girl! Is that understood?'

'Y-yes, Highness.'

He clapped his hands and a young, veiled servant appeared from the shadows. 'This is Amina,' he said briefly. 'She will settle you in and ensure that you have something suitable to wear.'

Pleased that his irritation seemed to have disappeared, Eleni gave an obedient nod. 'Thank you, Highness.'

His black eyes raked over her critically. 'And make sure you wash that straw out of your hair.'

Her cheeks still stinging, Eleni dropped to a deep curtsey but he had already swept out and her heart began to pound nervously. Didn't he realise how formidable he could be? How an inexperienced young woman could be daunted by the powerful mix of man and majesty?

Her fingers flew nervously to her hair. Did she really look such a fright, then? And she wasn't quite sure how she was supposed to judge. Appearance had never been number one on Eleni's list of priorities—there simply hadn't been the time, quite apart from anything else.

Amina led the way through the back of the palace and even though Eleni knew that these were the servants' quarters—it was still a brand-new experience for her. She could not imagine finding a scorpion here—or having to boot a rogue rat away from the back door.

And when at last Amina opened a door and indicated that Eleni should precede her, she thought that there must have been some kind of oversight.

'What…what is this?' she stumbled.

'This is your room,' said Amina, but Eleni shook her head and did not move.

'There must be some kind of mistake,' she told Amina as she took in the wide divan, the cool tiled floors and the intricate lamps which hung from the ceiling. Unshuttered windows looked out onto a serene rectangle of water where a fountain played soft, soothing music. It was like an illustration from one of those poetry books she used to read in school. The ones which used to send her off into an unachievable world of longing. Eleni swallowed. 'These can't be *my* quarters.'

Amina nodded. 'But they are.'

'And will I have to share the bed and the room with another servant?'

'No, Eleni,' said Amina gently. 'You are in the royal palace now and that means you are to have your own room.'

Eleni's heart beat faster with a kind of puzzled fear. 'But…but I am just his stable girl!'

Amina's expression remained closed. 'My role here is simply to obey instructions, not to question them,' she said. 'And since the sheikh values his horses more highly than diamonds themselves—those who tend them are also highly valued.'

Was Eleni being ultra-sensitive—or was there something which Amina wasn't telling her? 'Thank you,' she said uncertainly.

'And there are new clothes hanging over here in that tall cupboard. Come and take a look.'

Eleni blinked as the girl opened the door, for

surely this was a rail of clothes for twenty women and not just one? They were the typical Calistan tunic with slim-fitting trousers beneath—but these were made from silk, not the coarse cotton she was used to. And, like the rainbow which often followed the desert rains, Eleni had never seen so many hues—from vibrant to pale, with every shade in between.

'And I have drawn you a bath,' continued Amina.

Eleni stared at her. 'A bath?' she repeated blankly.

Amina pushed open yet another door and there, gleaming and steaming, was a large bath, set low into the ground and lined with gold. Eleni stood and gazed at it in dazzled fascination.

'By the falcon's wing!' she exclaimed. 'Who is this for?'

Amina gave a little smile. 'It is for you, Eleni,' she said gently. 'All for you.'

Eleni blinked, the unexpected sting of salt blurring her eyes. 'This is truly amazing,' she whispered in awe.

Amina nodded. 'I felt the same when first I was brought to the palace. Now, do you wish for me to assist you with your bathing?'

But if the thought of the bath was a daunting prospect, then the idea of getting naked in front of anyone made Eleni want to run a million miles in fear. 'Oh, no! Thank you, Amina—but I will manage by myself.'

Seeing the wide, square bath filled with scented water had dazed her, but more shocking still was Eleni's unexpected glimpse of herself in a mirror. How long since she had looked in a mirror? Not since school. Her father had banned them in the house as being indicators of vanity and there had seemed little need for her to gaze at herself.

But now she did and the sight which greeted her could not have been worse. Her face was engrained with desert dirt—and streaking over her cheeks were paler tracts where beads of sweat must have trickled down during the long, hot ride here. Her thick hair was dull and desperately in need of a wash and her clothes were covered with a fine layer of sand.

Eleni almost wept. Where was any trace of her femininity? Why, she looked more like a street urchin than a woman! With trembling fingers she pulled the dirty garments from her body—but as she turned she was confronted by another mirror and, in a way, this was even worse.

It was a full-length glass and she stared into it with a kind of horrified fascination at an Eleni she didn't recognise. How rounded her little breasts looked—and how pink their tips. She had not realised how curved her body had become—or that her waist was as tiny as the trunk of a young walnut tree. And there was more, too...

For the first time she could see the dark triangle of hair which lay at the fork of her thighs and she shrank back in fear, resolutely turning her back on the image to climb into the bath. She let the warm water glide over her aching limbs with a sense of relief.

And disbelief.

Because this was Eleni's first real taste of luxury and once again she almost wept, only this time with sheer joy, wondering how any experience could feel so utterly pleasurable.

She had learnt to find her enjoyment in simple things—like the feel of the wind on her hair when she was riding Nabat or the sight of a particularly beautiful sunset, sinking over the mighty splendour of the mountain. But this felt different. It felt…

Restlessly, Eleni stirred as ripples of water tickled at her skin and picked up the beautifully scented bar of soap. Her washing usually consisted of a hasty early-morning cold-water scrub in the outhouse while the rest of the world was sleeping. Yet just the touch of this soap was…was…

She swallowed as it foamed up into a

creamy cascade of foam over her skin and she felt the oddest sensation as she tentatively stroked some onto her breast. A face swam into her mind. A dark, mocking face with hard black eyes and cruel, curving lips.

The soap dropped into the water with a splash and as Eleni hauled herself out of the bath with flailing and slippery limbs she couldn't seem to stop herself from trembling.

CHAPTER FOUR

NEXT morning, Eleni arrived at the stable block soon after sunrise. Her first night's sleep at the palace had been restless, probably because of the rich food she'd been given for dinner in the staff kitchen—food which she had been astonished to discover she was not expected to cook for herself.

Eleni had never been waited on in her life. Nor felt soft silk against her skin when she had worn some of her new clothes down to supper. But before she had bedded down for the night, she had washed out her old things—more out of habit than anything else. She had hung them out on a rail in the bathroom and put them on this morning.

That way she felt more comfortable. More like herself.

With a spring in her step she greeted Nabat, who came whinnying up to greet her.

'Hello, boy,' she murmured. '*You* look happy!' She mucked him out and then exercised him—and while he was eating his oats—went over to look at all the sheikh's other horses. They were, as she might have expected, all utterly magnificent—but the finest of all was a huge black stallion at the far end of the yard. It was Kaliq's horse! The one he had ridden into her father's yard, the first time she'd seen him.

She could see that he was aristocratic and highly strung and at first he stared at her with suspicious eyes. But she approached him softly and calmly and after a few moments he started to nuzzle her in an impatient and friendly manner.

'Hello, my lovely,' she said softly as she ran her fingers appreciatively over his neck. 'You are *so* beautiful. Nearly as beautiful as Nabat—though we shall never allow *him* to hear me say that!'

But a soft sound in the yard disturbed her and Eleni turned round to see the sheikh standing very still, just watching her, and she swallowed, her heart beginning to race in an erratic, unsteady beat. It was the face from her dreams—which had kept sleep so tantalisingly at bay all night. The face which had flitted in and out of her mind when she had lain naked in her bath. Which had made her body feel so restless.

She swallowed as she drank in his dark beauty. Those black eyes. That ebony hair. Her eyes flickered downwards. And a lean body dressed in clothes which were unmistakably *western* today.

Eleni was so taken aback that she simply stared at the vision he made. He was wearing a tight, tight pair of trousers, a white silk shirt and long, leather boots. Never in her life had she seen a man dressed so…so *inappropriately*. Why, you could almost see the hard definition of his thighs and their powerful, curving muscles.

Her heart was beating wildly now—so wildly that for a moment Eleni felt quite lightheaded. She could feel the colour flaming in her cheeks as she went to curtsey to him, but he waved his hand impatiently.

'You like my horse, lizard?' he questioned silkily.

Horses were her passion—her reason for being here—so she must drive from her mind the terrible fascination of seeing the sheikh in these distracting garments. Concentrate on the question, she told herself fiercely. 'He is magnificent, Highness.'

'Yes. But temperamental, too. It is unusual for him to let a stranger so close. Very unusual.' His black eyes were hooded, and watchful. 'Think you can ride him?' he suggested silkily.

Eleni wasn't sure how to respond. Was this a challenge? A test to see whether she was intimidated by mounting such a mighty and valuable animal? But it seemed that he meant it, for he was interlocking his fingers together for her to use as a stirrup and nodding, she swung up on the horse's bare back without another word.

For a few seconds, she sank against the animal's powerful warm flesh, almost letting herself melt into it—to give both horse and rider confidence. Briefly, she saw the sheikh's black eyes narrow in astonishment as she began to trot the stallion around the yard as if she had spent her life riding him. But that was something which seemed to happen to her around horses—something magical and inexplicable which went some way to making up for the fact that it was always humans who seemed to let you down.

Eleni put the horse through its paces as she took him round, knowing that she was showing off a little—but who could blame her when Kaliq's critical gaze was searing over her like black fire? When had she last felt this good? This confident?

As Kaliq stood and watched her braided hair streaming behind her he felt the stir of recognition which was even fiercer then the sharp stir of desire. Because he recognised that he was witnessing something rare—the potent combination of talent, instinct and sheer bravado. And executed by a woman, too! His mouth flickered into a fleeting smile as she brought the horse to a halt beside him, bending down over the horse's neck and smiling straight into his face.

'Want me to jump him for you?' she questioned, exhilaration momentarily making her forget just who she was speaking to.

'Think you can?' he challenged as the spark of genuine excitement in her green eyes made him respond with equal candour.

'Oh, yes!'

The sound of a distant shout reluctantly brought Kaliq back into real time. Why, for a second then he had been so dazzled by her horsemanship that he had forgotten that she was nothing but a humble stable girl. Why, he had forgotten that she *was* a girl.

But now he noticed how the faint sheen of sweat clung to her skin, making her tunic stick to the curves of her body—undeniably emphasising her femininity. In fact, she was *not* a girl. Not at all. This green-eyed servant with the honeyed skin was pure woman.

Suddenly, he felt the insistent clamouring of sexual hunger. A sudden ache in response to the provocation in her confident assurance that she would be able to jump his powerful horse—a provocation made more sensual still by the fact that it was completely unintended.

Kaliq's mouth dried. 'Not now,' he said huskily. 'Dismount.'

Something dark which underpinned his aristocratic voice reminded Eleni exactly where she was. And that what she had just done surely amounted to a punishable offence…for she had been speaking to the Prince Kaliq Al'Farisi as if he were an *equal!*

It was as if the world had suddenly changed from safe to danger in the blinking of an eye. Aware of a strange and sudden tension hovering around them, Eleni slid to the ground. With trembling fingers she tied the stallion to a post and then stared up at the sheikh, dreading what he would think of her behaviour.

Kaliq stared at her, the pulsing of blood thick in his veins. 'You have a gift,' he said simply.

Eleni let out a low sigh of relief. So he wasn't angry that she had spoken to him as if she had been speaking to a stable lad! 'Thank you, Highness.'

A gift he must utilise, he thought, and then ran his eyes over her again—this time trying to ignore the soft swell of her hips and the lush pertness of her breasts. Despite the sheen of her newly washed hair—how could he take her anywhere when she still looked like the scruffy urchin he had found in her hovel of a desert home? 'You have settled into your quarters?' he questioned acidly.

'Yes, Highness.'

'And?'

'They are indeed the most beautiful—'

He cut across her words with an impatient wave of his hand. 'Please do not state the obvious,' he snapped. 'I have a whole palace of people who do that constantly—and it bores me. I ordered that new clothing was to be left there for you—yet today you appear before me dressed in this *lowly* apparel. Why is that? Do you reject my generosity?'

'No, Highness.'

'What, then?'

Inwardly, Eleni squirmed. 'It was just…'

'Just what?'

The ebony light from his black eyes was piercing. How could she tell him that the feel of fine silk brushing against her skin had made her feel peculiar—and not like herself at all. Just as he did. 'Habit, I suppose,' she answered instead.

'Then break it,' he ordered softly. 'When you work for a prince, you will dress accordingly, is that understood?'

'Yes, Highness.'

Idly, he ran the flat of his hand over his narrow hip. 'Really, you should be wearing jodhpurs,' he mused. 'Like these.'

It was impossible to avert her eyes from the cream-covered fabric which stretched almost indecently across his narrow hips and hugged the muscular thighs, but Eleni's natural modesty and fear made the words tumble out of their own accord. 'I could not possibly wear such garments as those, Highness!'

'No?' He thought that the soft rose flush of her cheeks made her green eyes look even more magnificent. Would she be as good in bed as she was in the saddle? he wondered, and was punished with another sharp spear of desire. 'Maybe not,' he agreed, on a sultry murmur, and felt his throat dry with lust.

Trying to dispel the image of how her bottom might look when hugged by a snug pair of jodhpurs, he forced his thoughts back to the present. 'Now listen to me. I have matters which I wish to discuss with you,' he said huskily. 'You will be brought to me later this evening.'

Brought to him? Eleni shifted from one foot to the other. 'Could we not…discuss it now?' she ventured, suddenly nervous.

He slammed her a chilly look. 'I said *tonight*, not now. You will follow my time-table,' he clipped out. 'Not your own. Do you understand?'

'Yes, Highness.'

'Good.' And with that, he untied the black stallion and leapt up onto its back, his hand tangled in its mane as he urged it forward with a swift clench of his powerful thighs.

In a daze, Eleni watched as he galloped off

in a cloud of dust, but for once her mind was far too preoccupied to be able to appreciate his amazing riding technique. Why did he want her brought to him tonight? And why had he made his summons sound not only imperious—but also, vaguely… Eleni swallowed. Not *threatening*, no—that would be too strong a description. But unsettling, yes—definitely unsettling—and she wasn't quite sure why.

But she didn't have the luxury of time spent in careless thought. There was too much to do and learn and so she set about discovering as much as she could about her new place of employment.

She was gratified to discover that the stable staff were far more welcoming than she had expected—though they seemed a little bemused at having a female in their midst. But then she was used to working mainly in isolation—with nothing but the occasional interference from a cruel and harsh father—and it made a welcome change to have a little company.

A day spent with horses always flew as fast as the hunting falcon—but here there was the added bonus of having the very finest facilities imaginable. Eleni felt as if she had died and gone to heaven.

She took Nabat out onto the gallops—accompanied by an eager young stable lad who, rather flatteringly, copied everything she did!

But even as the hours slipped away in a satisfying stream of tasks, Eleni was aware of a slow build up of dread and as she walked back to her rooms her heart was beating fast. As she ran the tip of her tongue over lips which had suddenly grown dry the thought she had spent most of the day trying to suppress came swimming to the forefront of her mind.

Tonight, she was to be brought to the sheikh, and she knew not why.

Amina had run a scented bath for her and afterwards, with Kaliq's critical assessment of her clothes still ringing in her ears, Eleni selected a gown from the stack hanging in the cupboard. Opting for the most unobtrusive shade she could find—a sort of quiet, silvery-grey—she slipped into the silky robe and braided her hair with a matching ribbon. But when she opened the door to Amina's gentle tap, it was disconcerting to see the servant bite back a small gasp of astonishment.

'Something is wrong?' questioned Eleni anxiously.

'No. Not at all. You look… Oh, you look *beautiful*, Eleni,' breathed Amina. 'You will indeed please the sheikh with your appearance.'

'But…but that's not what I intended!' Eleni blurted out. 'I mean, obviously I want to please him with my care of his horses, but not for anything else.'

Amina looked at first startled and then faintly disapproving. 'Do you not know that your own wishes are like breath on the wind?' she queried softly. 'Invisible to the eye and gone in an instant. The wishes of the Prince Kaliq are paramount in his palace—and he likes to look upon lovely things. Now come with me and come quickly—for one thing he does *not* like is to be kept waiting.'

What an all-powerful and controlling tyrant he sounded, thought Eleni, with a sinking heart. Why, he sounded no different from her own father—just royal and much richer! Her heart had begun to speed up and her palms were growing clammy as she followed Amina through a maze of cool, marble corridors which grew progressively grander with each passing step. Intricate woven metal lamps lit their way and cast flickering shadows, while the warm air was thick with blossom from the courtyard gardens.

At last Amina halted outside an imposing set of carved doors where two guards stood and she turned to Eleni with a soft expression on her young face. 'I must leave you now,' she whispered as one of the guards began to open the doors with a certain amount of ceremony. 'Good luck.'

Eleni could see the glittering interior as the doors yawned open and at that moment she felt more like five years old than twenty-five. A terrible mixture of dread and fear mixed with hope and excitement began to tingle over her.

And drawing in a deep breath, Eleni held her head high as she was summoned to the sheikh.

CHAPTER FIVE

IN THE vast royal dining chamber Kaliq lay back on a heap of embroidered cushions, wearing robes which shimmered like spun gold beneath the guttering light of tall candles. On a low table before him stood a heavy goblet which he looked as if he were about to lift, when he looked up and saw her.

And in that split second Eleni forgot why she was there and why she found herself in such an extraordinary situation. Forgot everything—including her sanity—as her heart did a curious flip. Ebony eyes glittered as they stared at her and a mouth which must surely define sin itself quirked into a mocking kind of smile. For a moment she felt so faint, so weak, so utterly *awed* by his royal presence that she was grateful that protocol demanded she curtsey to him. But her cheeks were still flushed when she straightened up again.

Kaliq hadn't moved; he hadn't dared to—for the arrow of desire had made a stiff rod to lie aching at his groin. One of his ancestors might well have snapped his fingers and called her over to pleasure him with her mouth, but such behaviour was no longer approved of within royal circles—even in Calista. He sighed. It had been a dark day when his stepmother Anya had first brought some sort of equality to the women of this island!

'Well, well, well,' he murmured. 'Let me look at you.'

'Highness?'

'Stand there.'

Kaliq's mouth hardened as his gaze swept over her. In many ways it was not a promising appearance. She had tied back that magnificent mane of hair like a schoolgirl and her face remained scrubbed free of all artifice. Not only that, but she had chosen possibly the most neutral shade of all—when most women with colouring like hers would have opted for something vibrant. Something green and lush to echo the colour of her incredible eyes.

And yet it really was extraordinary how she had emerged like a Venus from the waves now that all the desert dust had been washed away from her grimy little face. The rough clothes favoured by her people had been replaced by a fine silk which accentuated the fine curves of her fit and youthful body. Why, his little lizard looked almost beautiful!

He shifted his position so that the ache at his groin grew slightly more bearable.

'I believe that this is what they would call the "makeover",' he observed.

Eleni blinked. 'I do not understand what you mean, Highness.'

'No. I don't suppose you do.' His eyes glittered with mischief. 'In the west, women sometimes take their clothes off for the television cameras—have you ever seen television, lizard?'

'Once,' she admitted. It had been a crackly old set hung on the wall of a café near to where she and her father had taken Nabat to race and she had not been very impressed with the raucous game-show which had had most of the other customers screaming with laughter.

'And did you like it?' he demanded.

'Not particularly, Highness, no.'

'Those in the west are addicted to it,' Kaliq observed wryly. 'And allow the cameras to take many liberties with their lives. These women in the makeover programmes allow other women to poke their naked flesh and tell them what to wear.'

Despite her disapproval that the sheikh should have been watching such a programme, Eleni couldn't help herself. 'Please,' she protested. 'You must not joke with me, Highness!'

'But I do not joke.' A mocking smile curved

at his lips but the chauvinist within him silently applauded her entirely predictable reaction and the fact that she made no attempt to hide her rather prudish disapproval. How rare it was to find an unsophisticated woman—particularly for a man who moved within such rarefied social circles and globe-trotted as often as Kaliq did. He had only recently returned from Argentina—where he had been playing hard and fast on the polo field.

Afterwards, he had flown on to Rio where he had played even harder in the arms of a lover who was always exclusively available for him whenever he wanted her to be. And sometimes it was easier to take up with a woman you already knew than have to go through the mind-numbing motions of getting to know someone new.

The lady in question had possessed a dynamite body which she had delighted in flaunting. He found himself remembering her spectacular breasts, shown off in all their glory by the side of a swimming pool—and the pert thrust of her buttocks barely concealed by a shiny scarlet thong.

But although Kaliq was as appreciative of beauty and sexuality as the next man—wasn't there something deliciously refreshing about this young woman's genuine shock and outrage? His eyes flicked over her pink cheeks and pale green eyes. As well as something deliciously pleasing. His brows narrowed into a thoughtful look. What would she be like in his bed? he wondered idly. Would she be outraged at some of the things he would like to do to her—or would she embrace them with as much skill as she showed in the saddle?

He patted the cushions beside him. 'Come. Sit. You will eat.'

'Eat? You mean, here?' Eleni swallowed. 'With you?'

'But of course.' He glimmered her a smile. 'We must discuss my plans for the horses and there is no reason why we should not do so in comfort.'

'But—'

'Please do not argue with me,' he drawled, though his tone was emphatic. 'The first time you express a doubt I might find it tolerable—but repeat it and it will quickly become tedious. Do you understand?'

Oh, she understood, all right. Spoilt, jaded sheikh used to getting his own way at all times! But Eleni kept her face impassive as she nodded. 'Yes, Highness.'

His black eyes were glittering like jet as he pointed at the cushions and, although Eleni felt as if her limbs had been turned into marble, somehow she managed to walk over and sit down beside him. For what choice did she have when the sheikh had commanded it? Tell him that she'd rather be eating with the other servants in the kitchen as she had last night? That no morsel of food would ever be able to pass her lips in his daunting presence?

As if on cue, servant after servant began to noiselessly appear, carrying plates of exquisite food—some of which Eleni had never seen before, let alone tasted. Alongside the usual meat curry there was rare fish from the waters of the Kordela river, and jewel-bright fruits laid out on gleaming platters of pure gold. There were nuts and sweets, too—of such a variety that were usually only seen on feast days and holidays.

But more disturbing still than the sight of such a lavish feast was the prince's proximity. Eleni could almost feel the warmth of his body beside her and was appalled by the way it made her heart race with a strange kind of excitement. She did not know what to do, or where to look. For if she cast her eyes downwards as was correct—then might he not once again remonstrate with her? And yet she could not bear to look directly into that forbiddingly aristocratic face—for fear that she would never be able to tear her gaze away from its dark beauty.

'Eleni.'

He had even remembered her name!

She looked directly into the ebony eyes, her heart giving that terrible little wrench again. 'Yes, Highness.'

'Come, come—you must be hungry. Stop staring into space and eat something,' he said softly. 'For you have had a long day in the stables.'

She couldn't possibly tell him that she had never felt less like eating in her life, could she? Might that not be seen as an insult to his hospitality? And anyway, not a morsel had yet passed *his* lips, though he was looking at her expectantly.

'But a man must always eat first and take his fill before a woman,' she protested as she tried and failed to imagine her father letting her have first choice of any food.

Kaliq frowned. And that, he realised—with a start—was the downside of inequality. He had never considered it before and for the first time in his life he saw that his late step-mother's fight to end sexual discrimination in Calista might not have been a bad thing. 'Eat,' he said softly. 'For your sheikh commands it.'

And didn't everyone know that a sheikh's wishes must be met? Self-consciously picking up a piece of fish, Eleni wrapped it in an edible leaf and began to eat and suddenly all her doubts and fears melted away in the wake of such a delicious explosion of tastes and flavours in her mouth. The sheikh had been right—she had ridden and worked since sunrise with nothing more than a handful of fruit in her belly. And this was like the food of the gods.

'It's good?' he questioned, almost indulgently.

'It's…it's wonderful.'

He watched while she ate, his eyes drawn to her with a rare fascination—thinking that everything she did was with a certain kind of grace.

But he was not employing her for her grace. He was employing her for her prowess with horses—but now Kaliq could see for himself that Eleni had other very commendable attributes, too. And surely it would be a crime not to avail himself of them? As the silvery silk rippled over her firm, young arm, he felt the first soft beat of anticipation.

Forcing himself to wait until she had finished eating, he clapped his hands and the dishes were removed—and then he dismissed the last of the guards and other servants who always lingered in the darkened alcoves in case he wished for something on a whim.

'Now,' said Kaliq softly.

Eleni's senses were alerted—but to what she knew not. Almost without meaning to, she shrank back slightly against the silken mound of cushions, stared up into the harsh yet beautiful face with its cruel curve of a nose and glittering black eyes.

'You wish to discuss horse welfare?' she questioned nervously.

Kaliq almost laughed—but he knew that

laughter had no place in the bedchamber. Horse welfare was the very last thing on his mind right now! So was she being prim, or merely cowed by his royal presence? He leaned towards her, seeing her green eyes darken. 'How old are you?' he questioned softly.

'Tw-twenty-five.'

Older than he had thought! 'Ah, that is good,' he purred as he lifted one of the braids of hair and rubbed his fingers experimentally over the thick, silken rope. 'Yet heading towards thirty and you've never had a husband?'

'Why, no, Highness.'

'Never wanted one?'

Eleni clamped her lips together. These were very personal and rather hurtful questions for her ruler to be asking—though she suspected that he wasn't really interested. She doubted whether he wanted to hear that the young men who had attempted to woo her had either been oafish, or had been chased away by a father reluctant to lose his unpaid servant. And why was he touching her hair like that? 'My life has been my horses,' she answered truthfully.

'How very commendable,' he murmured. 'But there is so much more to life than horses.'

There was absolutely nowhere to look but into the gleam of his eyes, which were dazzling her with ebony fire, seeming to suck away all the strength in her body, leaving her feeling defenceless beneath its powerful searchlight.

'Isn't there, Eleni?' he continued softly.

'I…' But Eleni had no time to put together a sentence—even if her brain hadn't just turned to honeycomb—because the unbeliev-able was now happening. Prince Kaliq Al'Farisi was lowering his dark and beautiful head and those mocking lips were moving towards her lips.

He was going to kiss her!

Eleni had never been kissed before and she was not to know that it was being executed by a master of the art. All she *did* know were a series of conflicting sensations which were dragging her into a sweetly erotic world she hadn't dreamed could exist. She could feel the silken seeking of his mouth and the instant clamouring of her senses in response. Could hear her heart beating so loud and so hard that she was afraid it might burst beneath her breast. And now a strange honeyed rush was beginning at the fork of her thighs, which had her almost choking with pleasure.

He was pressing against her now, pushing her down onto the cushions. Almost arrogantly, he had splayed his hand over one breast and—both shamefully and delightfully—Eleni could feel that breast reacting to his caress. It was growing full and tingly and achy—and, inexplicably, she found herself longing for him to touch it more, and much harder.

'Highness!' she gasped as she felt the royal tongue licking its way deliciously over her lips. 'Oh, Highness!'

'Mmm?'

Fighting every instinct in her body, Eleni detached her mouth. 'We must stop this,' she said weakly.

'No!' he growled, tiptoeing his fingers over the growing bud of her nipple and groaning as it peaked through the silk gown. Increasing the urgency of his mouth, he felt her lips open and Kaliq began to ruck the silk of her dress up over her ankles. Ah, the sweet firmness of her ankle with its soft, silken flesh! And beyond? What treasures lay undiscovered there? 'Not yet.'

'Yes!' Eleni knew little of the ways of love—her sexual education had been one hasty class at school and a peep at an ancient art-book shown to her by her favourite teacher before it had been confiscated by the school's head. She knew that sex was sacred, secret and forbidden—and yet, now she was sampling her first taste of it, she could see how tempting it was, too.

Kaliq was playing with her aching breast and sliding up her silken gown and she was lying there and just *letting him*—even though she knew it was wrong!

It was like dragging herself back from the edge of paradise, but Eleni knew she had to get herself out of such a dangerous situation with such a highly experienced and powerful man. Get out now—before it was too late.

With a strength she didn't know she possessed—a strength forged from years of hard, physical work in the stable—she pushed the sheikh away from her, surprising a series of conflicting emotions on his face as she did so.

She saw frustration and a dark smouldering kind of anger, but more than any of these things she saw astonishment.

'What in the falcon's name do you think you are doing?' he questioned, with silky menace.

Eleni's breathing was so erratic that it took a moment before she could speak, and even then, she felt odd—as if she were sickening for something. Dizzy. Disorientated. Her blood boiling in her veins and her head spinning.

'I am guarding my honour!' she cried out, not caring now about protocol.

Kaliq's mouth twisted. 'Your *honour*?' he questioned acidly, as if she had just invented a new word. 'What are you talking about?'

Eleni couldn't really move—and in truth she did not think she would be able to. But she knew that things needed to calm down and that somehow she must help the sheikh lose that look of pure fury on his face. Because surely once he understood the truth of her predicament—then he would understand?

'You do not think that I have a reputation that I guard fiercely?' she demanded hotly. 'That my honour is not worth preserving?'

'Your honour?' he echoed again as he tried to ignore the fierce throb of hunger which pulsed through his body.

'I may be a simple country girl—but even I know that such an act between two people who barely know one another would be wrong.'

Frustration made him want to ask her

whether she was holding out for dinner first—but he suspected that irony would be lost on her, quite apart from the fact that he bet she'd never been taken out for dinner in her life.

'But I, as your sheikh, want it,' he argued, quite reasonably. 'So how can it be wrong?'

Eleni took the opportunity to wriggle back a little on the bank of silk cushions, trying to steady her still-ragged breathing and wishing that her heart would slow down. But that fractional increase in the distance between them made all the difference.

'I would lose respect,' she said.

'Whose? Mine? I can assure you that your surrender will make me respect you more,' he murmured, lifting his hand to brush away a lock of silken hair which had escaped.

Eleni looked at him, trying to ignore the instinctive thrill she felt when he touched her. She didn't believe him, not for a moment. He reminded her of her favourite stable cat—a sleek and beautiful creature, but one who would happily trail after anyone who happened to feed her. But of course she would not do anything as stupid as calling the sheikh a liar.

'It would be unsuitable, Highness,' she continued implacably. 'And ultimately it might distract your attention from Nabat.'

For a moment he didn't have a clue what she was talking about, until he realised that she meant her wretched horse. For a moment he wanted to exclaim that the horse could go to hell for all he cared—that her sweet young body excited him far more—but even he recognised that this would not do his case any good.

Did she not realise that there wasn't a woman alive who had ever turned down the opportunity of such sensual pleasure with Prince Kaliq Al'Farisi? Did she not realise that there could be dire consequences from incurring his royal displeasure? Dropping his hand from the pure oval of her face, he gave a click of irritated frustration.

'I'm not interested in the damned horse!' he snapped, unable to stop himself.

Eleni's expression exhibited nothing but interested enquiry, even though her heart was racing like a piston beneath the expensive robe she wore. 'But I thought that was your reason for bringing me here, Highness.'

He met her innocent gaze with a frown. Was it simply his imagination—or was there a teasing challenge in the depths of those green eyes? If he told her that her courage and youth and arresting eyes had played their part in bringing her here—then would that not put him at a disadvantage? Did she not realise that he could have any woman he wanted and that she was lucky that he had deigned to pick *her*? Well, she would discover it soon enough!

'Then we will discuss the horses,' he drawled, stifling a yawn—as if he had grown bored with the conversation.

For a moment, Eleni wondered whether she had gone too far—but what choice did she have? She would have acted in the same way no matter who had attempted such a casual and quick seduction. And just because Kaliq was a sheikh did not mean that he should be treated any differently from any other man, did it?

It was true that no one else had ever made her feel like that—as if she had just discovered what a woman's body had been designed for—but surely that itself was dangerous? Imagine if she got used to a sheikh's caresses and began comparing everyone else to him. That, of course, presumed that there was ever going to *be* anyone else, which was looking increasingly unlikely as she headed unmarried towards thirty—as the sheikh himself had rather cruelly pointed out.

She gave him a bright smile. 'Does the sheikh not drink mint tea after dinner?' she questioned softly. 'I always find it very relaxing.'

For a moment Kaliq did not know whether to laugh or explode or whether to send the impudent minx packing back to her hovel of a home and her drunk of a father. But the challenge of her defiance was proving almost irresistible and he conceded that she did have a point and so he lifted his hands and clapped them to order tea.

But as he did so the silken sleeves of his robe fell back to reveal his arms and Eleni's eyes widened as she bit back a gasp. For there, just at his wrists, were deep, ugly and livid scars.

'Oh, Highness!' she exclaimed softly—all thwarted passion forgotten at the shocking sight of his injuries. 'Who has dared hurt you?'

CHAPTER SIX

WITHOUT thinking Eleni leaned forwards and brushed her fingertips over one of the angry red ridges which scarred both the sheikh's wrists and Kaliq's mouth tightened.

Truly, her impulsive gesture was an imposition—for how dared a commoner touch a prince in such a way? Yet considering he had been touching *her* only moments before—he was disinclined to stop her. Even if the feel of her breast was infinitely more pleasurable than the feel of her fingers. Although…

He frowned. Her touch was oddly distracting. It was soothing—almost healing. Was that why she was so wonderful with horses, he wondered—because she had the gift of softness about her? And if he allowed her this touch then wouldn't it lead them down the path of sensual pleasure? Only this time—with her sympathy engaged—she would be less likely to stop him. He gave a cynical half-smile. Women were very predictable.

'What happened?' she asked quietly, her fingertip automatically questing over one of the hardened and raised red ridges as she saw his black brows crease into a hard line.

'You are very impertinent, lizard,' he drawled. But he didn't move his hand away from the comforting caress. 'To ask your sheikh such a question.'

Biting her lip, she let his wrist go. 'Forgive me.'

But strangely her question did not trouble him as much as protocol demanded. Now why was that? Was it because women *always* asked about these marks—only he was usually naked when first they noticed them? And the scars on his back were much worse—making these seem almost trifling in comparison.

Sometimes he explained them away by saying that an over-enthusiastic partner had got slightly carried away during a sex-game. Sometimes they believed him—depending on their own experience and worldliness. Even when they clearly *didn't* believe him they rarely challenged him—because they were too busy clicking into whichever fantasy they thought he wanted from them. They tried to be everything he wanted in order to please him—and in so doing they ended up being nothing.

But Eleni was different. Probably because she was low-born. Did she not realise how preposterous it was for a humble stable girl to have tenderly stroked the raised weals at his wrists?

But perhaps your kiss made her think that all such contact was appropriate.

He studied her as suddenly her inexplicable refusal to allow him more than a kiss made sense. 'Are you a virgin?' he demanded.

She shrank back against the silken cushions. 'Highness!'

His black eyes glittered like jet. 'You asked me an impertinent question and now I am asking you one in return. What do you say— shall we exchange intimate knowledge, lizard? That seems only fair to me.'

Eleni bit her lip. It seemed a terribly personal thing for him to want to know—but perhaps if she told him then he might not try to seduce her again as he had done this evening.

Even if you want him to? taunted a voice in her head. *Even though the touch of his lips made you feel more alive than you've ever done in your life*?

Swamping down her rogue thoughts, she nodded her head reluctantly. 'Yes, I am a virgin, Highness,' she said quietly, her cheeks flaring scarlet.

Kaliq seized on the information with a feeling of triumph. So *that* was why she had done the unthinkable and resisted his advances. But he could feel the renewed beat of excitement, too. A virgin. A sweet, green-eyed virgin. How the gods must be looking down on him—and how good it would be to enjoy such a gift for his own.

'I cannot believe that you have never known a man's love,' he observed, his mouth drying at the thought of initiating her into the art of love-making. Of piercing through her tight maidenhood. Of having those soft breasts in his hands and those firm thighs wrapped tightly around his back. 'I thought that you country girls sometimes took lovers out of wedlock.'

'Perhaps some of them do, Highness, but not me,' said Eleni disapprovingly.

'Yet you might die and never know the pleasures of the body.'

'Then I will gladly accept my fate,' she answered fiercely.

He laughed at her feistiness. 'Ah, but you are missing out on a great deal, Eleni—one of the greatest wonders of life,' he said softly. 'More than you will ever know if you do not try it for yourself.'

His eyes had softened, as well as his voice, so that they were more like molasses than jet and again Eleni was reminded with shocking clarity just how potent his kiss had been. And that strange and bewitching sensation of the sheikh's tongue entering her mouth and…and…

'Perhaps what you say is true, Highness—but I will not attempt to control my own destiny by lying with a man. To seek to shed my virginity simply for the sake of it is not how a well-brought-up girl should behave!'

'And you are a well-brought-up girl, are you, Eleni?'

She heard the mockery in his voice and she wanted to tell him not to confuse her with her father—that her mother had brought her up to behave as much like a lady as was possible when living in such basic conditions. But, of course, she could not boast about her own qualities at the expense of her father's reputation.

'Yes, Highness, I am. I know the difference between right and wrong and if it is not meant to be, then I accept that. After all, no-one can possibly have everything in life,' she answered carefully. 'And since I've answered your question—is it not fair to now answer mine, Highness? How did you come by these terrible scars?'

How bold she was, he thought admiringly with a renewed kick of lust at his groin. And how outrageous of her to interrogate him in the light of her refusal to let him bed her. He could order her to go to hell…

But how long since he had talked about that terrible day when his world had changed for ever? It was a subject off-limits, even with his twin who shared the awful guilt. A dark secret which had been hushed up by the palace apparatus like so much else. A stain on the family of Al'Farisi.

Yet secrets became burdens which could grow in weight until they became intolerable— and suddenly the innocent and green-eyed young stable girl seemed as welcoming and as unthreatening as a newborn falcon chick.

'You know about my brother?' he demanded.

The royal family of Calista was an endless source of fascination to its people. Even without mass communication, gossip about the ruling clan was always available—it was swopped in the market place or spoken of outside the school gates, just as it was the world over.

Eleni knew that there had been five brothers—one of whom was his twin, Aarif. And she knew too that there was some terrible tragedy surrounding the youngest. Hadn't he gone missing—when he was just a child?

'You mean…Zafir?' she ventured nervously.

Kaliq flinched. She was one of his subjects, simply answering his question—yet it reso-nated painfully to hear Zafir's name spoken aloud and a pang of remorse shot through him. How long since he had thought of his black-eyed little brother?

Had he, and the palace, been guilty of air-brushing from their lives the tousle-haired young sheik who had disappeared at the age of six, lost without trace and never to be seen again? Was it because the painful reality had become too much for them all to bear—or were they emotional cowards who simply pushed away the darker sides of life?

Yet Kaliq was not a man usually given to soul-searching and he stared at the young stable girl angrily, blaming her for the sharp stir of memory.

'What do you know of Zafir?' he demanded.

Eleni wondered what had caused his hard black eyes to cloud over with such terrible pain that she wanted to take his injured wrist in her hand and rub it again, as she would a horse who had been pierced by a deep thorn—but she did not dare for all kinds of reasons.

'I know that something terrible happened to him,' she answered with slow truth.

Black eyes pierced into her. 'But you do not know what?'

'Our history lessons at school…they were very basic, Highness.' Eleni remembered one of her father's card-playing companions—a wild poet who had drunk an entire flagon of *Zelyoniy* by himself during a game of poker. What had he said? That the people knew only what the palace wished them to know. Censorship, he had called it—but Eleni remembered thinking at the time that keeping the dark stuff secret was just being private, surely? The sort of thing that any family might do—especially for a family in the spotlight as much as the royals were. 'What happened to him, Highness?'

Her soft voice wove into the cold stone of his memory. How long since he'd said it aloud? 'My twin brother and I took a raft out to sea,' he said flatly, as memories of that nightmare day came back, as bitterly sharp as if it had happened yesterday. 'And Zafir begged to come along with us. We were supposed to be looking after him, you see. Neither of my other brothers were around, and so we were responsible for him. We should have left him at home—by the raven's claw we *should* have left him at home, but…'

'Little boys can be very persistent,' interjected Eleni softly.

And very appealing, thought Kaliq—as he remembered the child's winning smile. Was it because their mother had died giving birth to him and because he had never known the comfort or security of a mother's love that everyone had made allowances for Zafir, who had quickly learned he could wrap anyone around his cute little finger?

'The raft was swept out to sea,' he remembered slowly. 'And we were captured by some scum diamond smugglers—and in the course of the struggle, little Zafir blurted out that they had taken three royal sheikhs as prisoners.'

'Which would have been a far more lucrative bounty than all the diamonds in Calista,' breathed Eleni with horror—as she imagined the delight of the smugglers when they discovered the unexpected value of their captives. 'Oh, Highness—what happened?'

Kaliq barely noticed the familiarity of her question. It seemed that he was on a roll now—as if he had unleashed a dark torrent of facts which were determined to stream from his lips like poison. 'Zafir managed to free us from the ropes which bound us and we quickly put him on the raft—but as we were following him our escape was noticed. We were shot at—Aarif got hit in the face. He fell into the sea and I dived in to save him. Naturally, we were recaptured.'

'And…Zafir?'

Kaliq flinched, clenching his hands into two tight fists. 'The raft drifted away—and with it

Zafir. No trace of him has ever been found— despite the longest and most intensive searches put in place by my father. That was the last anyone ever saw of him. He was six years old,' he repeated, his mouth twisting with pain.

Eleni stared at him in horror. 'And what happened to you and your twin brother if you were still prisoners?'

'Oh, they thrashed us and nearly killed us…' His mouth twisted. 'Sometimes I wish that they had—'

'Highness! You should never wish that.'

'Better that I should have perished if my little brother could have been found,' he flared back, and as the old rage and despair came back to assail him he glared at her, even angrier now that she had been the one to instigate this. To make him feel this pain again, when he had locked it deep inside him for so long. He would teach her to pry. He would teach her everything!

He reached for her and her green eyes

widened like one of the palace cat's as he stared down at her. 'You will kiss me,' he grated. 'You will not deny me that.'

Eleni knew that she dared not refuse him but the truth was that she didn't want to—for written on his face was so much more than mere desire. There was pain and bitterness and a deep self-loathing, too. He blamed himself for his little brother's disappearance, she realised achingly—even though he had been little more than a boy himself. And somehow she saw that human contact was what this powerful autocrat craved at this moment more than anything. *And you crave it too, Eleni. At least admit* that.

She bit her lip. Surely no harm could come of one simple kiss—for instinctively she felt that the sheikh would not dare to take her by force. Or was she being too trusting?

She touched her fingertips to the harsh line of his mouth, wanting above all else to see it soften and smile. 'Yes, Highness,' she said quietly. 'I give you permission to kiss me.'

In spite of his anguish and frustrated longing Kaliq almost laughed aloud at the gross impertinence of this lowly stable girl giving him—*him the sheikh*—permission to kiss her!

But her lips were too soft and inviting for remonstration. Too beguiling for her own good. And yet instead of driving his own down hard on them as a preliminary to taking her swiftly and without ceremony—Kaliq found himself exercising an unknown restraint. Was that because this whole situation was so bizarre? He was a man whose appetite was jaded by excess and the unusual had the power to captivate him—who could blame him for wanting to prolong it?

First he traced the outline of her lips with the tip of his finger before following it with the brush of his mouth. He grazed his lips over hers almost negligently—feeling them tremble like a heat-haze in response. And strangely, Kaliq found himself luxuriating in the slow sensuality of this meeting of flesh. At the realisation that this was the first time a man had ever kissed her. And the oddly haunting recognition that he couldn't remember a kiss feeling quite this good before.

Because he had never bedded a virgin—and maybe they needed to be treated differently. Perhaps he needed to take his time with her— just as you would take time to saddle up a nervous mare before jumping her.

'Eleni,' he said softly.

'H-highness.'

Pushing her further into the soft heap of cushions, he took her face in between the palms of his hands and stared at her long and hard before kissing her again, with a soft intent he had never used before. Just enough to provoke but not enough to frighten her. And he could not deny that he was intoxicated by her response.

Her lips were velvety and completely untutored and yet he could sense the instinctive eagerness which lay behind her innocence.

No doubt the same sound instinct she demonstrated with horses. Could he capitalise on her purity and his experience? Kiss her into submission until she was so senseless with desire that she would let him have his way with her?

He drew his mouth away, noting the flush to her cheeks and the darkened pools of her eyes—the way that her breath had quickened. And suddenly Kaliq realised that it would be far more exciting if he seduced her to the point of mindless longing—until she *begged* him to take her. What a prize that would be!

'You like being kissed by me, Eleni?' he questioned idly.

Dazzled by the tumult of her feelings and dazed by the candid look he was piercing at her, Eleni bit her lip. What an unnecessary question—and how could she possibly answer it? By saying that his kiss was the most wonderful thing which had ever happened to her? That it made her want to open her heart to him, as well as her body. Because that would be true. But something warned Eleni to stick to facts, not feelings—for the sheikh did not want to hear fervent declarations of emotion from a humble stable girl.

'Yes, Highness,' she said softly.

His black eyes blazed into her. 'How lukewarm your praise!' he mocked.

Her gaze flickered uncertainly to his glittering black eyes. 'I liked it very much.'

Her shy acclaim was oddly moving, and Kaliq's mouth twisted. Unless she was playing the games that women often did—acting coy in order to appeal to his sense of honour. But he did not think she was playing games—apart from anything else, games had to be learned, and what could her life so far have possibly taught her other than how to mount and train a horse?

The thought of her mounting a horse—of the muscular flesh of the animal locked between her soft thighs—made him grow harder still, but Kaliq quickly came to a decision. There would be no sex here tonight—not without a lot of effort on his part—that much was clear. So there was little point in her hanging around kissing him on the silken cushions.

But he wanted her—and he would have her. He just needed to work out how best to go about it.

'Go now and rest,' he said dismissively, and then a slow smile began to curve his cruel lips as he began to get the first shimmering of an idea which would throw a little excitement and unpredictability into the mix. 'We will need to talk in the morning about our trip.'

Eleni had been scrambling to her feet—half pleased to have been granted her freedom and yet half disappointed that the prince had decided against kissing her again. But his words drew her up short and she stared down at him.

'Trip, Highness? Wh-what trip would that be?'

'Didn't I tell you?' he drawled carelessly. 'I am going to Europe—and I am taking you with me.'

CHAPTER SEVEN

ELENI quickly learned that if a royal sheikh did not wish to speak to you, then there was little point in trying to pursue a conversation with him. And that a royal sheikh certainly never considered that he needed to explain his behaviour.

So that last night, when she had turned to Prince Kaliq to ask him what on earth he meant by proposing to take her to *Europe*—he had simply waved his hand in an arrogant gesture of dismissal. And then his retinue had arrived as if he had sent out some silent summons—before the whole lot of them had disappeared in a swish of glimmering robes.

Leaving Eleni to make her way back to her

room and spend the night tossing and turning in her soft palace bed while her mind spun with possibilities and confusion.

Europe he had said. Had he been playing some kind of joke on her? What possible reason could there be to go into a faraway region she had only seen represented on the pages of her geography books? Frowning, she tried to remember—but geography had seemed a pointless subject to embrace when she had known that she was unlikely ever to leave the shores of Calista. Was Madrid the capital of Spain, or was that Barcelona? she wondered. And was England the country which looked like a resting grasshopper?

Despite her restless night, she was up at dawn to muck out and exercise Nabat, and rode him long and hard over the gallops— and the wind in her face briefly blew away all her worries. Once she'd fed him, she poured herself some of the strong coffee which one of the stable lads brought out. Then she took the tin mug and a large orange and went and sat on a low wall overlooking the gallops, watching the sun rising over the distant mountains while she peeled and ate the fruit.

At first she didn't hear the footfall behind her, so lost was she in thought. In fact, it wasn't until a silky voice said her name that she jumped—her mouth so full of orange that for a moment she couldn't speak as she scrambled down off the wall to face Kaliq.

Today, he was wearing his traditional flowing robes—so at least she was spared the distracting sight of his jodhpurs—and his dark gaze was mocking as it swept over her in swift assessment.

Kaliq's mouth twisted. Her braided hair was escaping its ribbons—presumably because she'd been out on her horse—and she was again wearing those drab riding clothes. Her green eyes dominated her bare face and yet her full mouth was shiny and sticky from the fruit she was eating. No woman could have looked more unexpectedly provocative, he thought achingly—and yet no woman of his acquaintance would have been quite so oblivious to that fact.

'Good morning, Eleni,' he said silkily. 'Did you sleep well?'

She managed a curtsey. 'Good morning, Highness,' she said, ignoring his question for fear of where it might lead.

'How's Nabat?'

'He is truly contented in his new home,' she said truthfully.

'I saw one of the lads petting him just now.' He saw her start and a sardonic smile curved his lips. 'Calm down, lizard—you won't be doing the creature any favours if you try to make him completely dependent on you.'

'But he is!'

'That's not true and you know it. He favours you,' he admitted slowly. 'And he always will. But give him a bucket of oats and a clean stable and he will be a happy horse.' His black eyes studied her. 'Because he's going to have to get used to being without you for a few days. Remember what I said to you last night?'

Eleni shook her head, trying to dispel the imagery his question had produced. He had said and done a lot of things last night and every single one of them made her feel uncomfortable when she thought about them this morning. 'Highness, no,' she whispered.

'You are surely not objecting to your sheikh taking you to Europe? Why, most women would give up everything they owned for such an opportunity,' he murmured, enjoying watching her struggle with her emotions until she could contain them no more.

'I cannot come to Europe with you, Highness,' she breathed.

'Why not?'

'Because…because it would not be proper.'

'Proper?' he echoed.

Unable to see the trap he was setting for her,

Eleni nodded. 'Surely it would give rise to gossip, Highness.'

Dark eyebrows were elevated in mocking query. 'You are perhaps concerned with the sleeping arrangements, while I think only of horses—ah, but how swiftly our roles have been reversed, lizard. You think that my subjects will imagine that the Prince Kaliq Al'Farisi lies with his stable girl?'

Eleni felt the beginnings of a blush begin to flare at her face. Put like that it *did* sound laughable. 'I did not mean—'

'It is not your place to tell me what is *proper*. It is not your place to tell me anything. And I am not *asking* you to come with me to Europe, I am *commanding* you!' he snapped. 'As it happens, there is a polo pony in England which I'm thinking of buying to bring back to the club here. And I want your advice.'

'But—' Eleni swallowed down the word and looked down at the ground, furious now. How dared he take liberties with her last night on his embroidered cushions and this morning snap at her to accompany him to England as if she were some kind of lapdog!

'But what, Eleni?'

Reluctantly, she lifted her gaze, wondering if her anger had completely disappeared—though part of her didn't care if he saw it. 'Nothing, Highness.'

He noted the sparks which were spitting from the pistachio eyes. 'No. I want to know.'

'I thought it was not my place to offer an opinion,' she offered.

Kaliq's eyes narrowed. Was she *mocking* him? No, of course not. She wouldn't dare. 'Tell me,' he instructed silkily.

'I know nothing about polo ponies.'

'Maybe not, but you have an instinct about horses—a sound instinct which I trust.' His eyes narrowed into ebony shards of jet. 'You should not have showed off quite so much on my stallion yesterday if you did not wish me to capitalise on your expertise. The horse for sale is one of the most expensive in the world—and I want you to use that instinct to tell me whether or not I should buy him.'

She wanted to point out that he had only just acquired a horse—Nabat—so why on earth was he looking to buy another? But, of course, Nabat was not an experienced polo pony—he just happened to be a race-winner among his own particular Arabian breed. And she knew that Kaliq had invested much of his own personal fortune in modernising the polo club on Calista—so presumably he needed to build up a winning stable of his own.

Eleni suddenly recognised that, as well as royal princes being spoiled by possessions and wealth, here was a man with a very low threshold of boredom. One horse was never enough—why, give him a hundred horses and he would probably still seek the one he did not have! And even if his polo club became the most famous in the world—that would probably fail to satisfy him, too.

If she'd had the freedom to speak her mind then she might have told him so, and to hell with the consequences. Even if he kicked her off the royal land—then surely she could find herself some sort of gainful employment to put bread in her mouth.

But as well as being fearful of launching out on her own—in a world where she had always been relatively protected—she would also have to leave Nabat behind. No, she was trapped in this bizarre situation as surely as the wounded hare over which the falcon circled…

And then she remembered some of the things the sheikh had said to her last night— when he hadn't been kissing her. She remembered the fierce, harsh look of pain which had momentarily transformed his face into a bitter mask and she felt herself melt in spite of her misgivings. Had the tragic loss of his brother and the subsequent guilt made him into the man he was today? A man who did not really know what it was he was looking for? And should she not take that into account when dealing with him—for surely there could be a corner of kindness in her heart for this privileged and yet wounded man?

'I do not have a passport,' said Eleni primly, and Kaliq threw his dark head back, and laughed.

'You think that is going to be a problem for the companion of a sheikh?' he drawled.

'No, I suppose not,' she agreed. But she wanted to ask him if he didn't ever wish that it *was*. Didn't he ever yearn for the constraints and problems of the ordinary person?

'Your passport will be arranged,' he said silkily and his eyes roved lazily over her. 'But you will need clothing more suited to the West.'

Protectively, Eleni's hand strayed to her well-worn riding top. 'I appreciate that this would be unsuitable—but you have already provided me with an extensive wardrobe of fine clothes, for which I thank you, Highness. And I promise that from now on I shall wear them all the time—'

'But you might wish to wear different clothes in Europe,' he said bluntly.

'Do *you*?' she challenged.

He laughed. 'No, I do not—but I am the sheikh who can behave however he wishes, and you are nothing but a stable girl. The world of polo in Europe is quite unlike anything you will have ever dreamed of, Eleni. You will be moving among some of the wealthiest and most cosseted women in the world, and perhaps would prefer to blend in. Dress like that and you will be patronised.'

Eleni shook her head in denial. 'The attitude of other women will not concern me,' she said proudly. 'For I am a decent Calistan woman, and I cannot show my flesh in public!'

'And you will not,' he agreed. 'But there are more alluring ways of covering your body than by wearing these traditional garments. Oh, and, Eleni?'

'Highness?'

'Let us be very clear on one thing. You may

be decent and you are certainly from Calista and you may look like a woman, but you are not one yet.' He paused. 'You are still a girl,' he added softly.

How stupid could she have been not to have interpreted the gleaming light of intent in his black eyes as he uttered these somehow damning words? Or seen the hand which snaked out like a cobra to snare her and bring her crushing up against him?

And despite the loose-fitting silken garment he wore—Eleni could feel every sinew and hard muscle beneath, almost as if, as if…

'Yes,' he said softly as he saw the colour begin to rise in her cheeks and felt the sudden change as her body stiffened with awareness. 'Did you not know that royal princes do not like to be constrained? I am naked beneath my robes!'

'Highness!' It was as if he had read her thoughts. Oh, but she prayed that he couldn't! Because then he might get some kind of inkling of how…how…*exciting* she found his embrace. How tantalising she found his closeness.

Dizzily, she swayed, aware of some raw and heady scent coming from his warm male body and, despite her total lack of experience with the opposite sex, she knew enough to realise that this was desire, pure and simple. And didn't she feel an answering desire—as memories of his sweet kiss filled her body with longing?

He brought his lips up close to her ear and his breath was warm, too. Warm and as enticing as a soft, summer breeze and she gave a sigh.

'Ah, Eleni,' he said softly. 'Shall I dismiss the stable staff and take you over to a quiet corner and make you into a woman here and now? Believe me, you will never get a better offer. Your sheikh showing you all the pleasures of the body which are all there, just for the taking. Just slide your hand up underneath my robe and feel how hard I am for you.'

'Highness!' she gasped.

'Was that supposed to be a protest?' he taunted silkily as his mouth moved down to graze along the slim column of her neck. 'Because if so, you need to put a little more feeling into it to convince me.'

'I...I...' Her throat was so parched that the sounds she made sounded like a dry leaf being crunched underfoot. *Just kiss me*, she thought—even though she despised herself for wanting it. *Just please kiss me the way you did last night.*

Sensing her longing, Kaliq was tempted to take her. To have done with the hunger and, by so doing, to rid himself of it. But it would be a bore to have to first clear the stable—and it would be bound to incite talk among the staff, no matter how much they feared the consequences of idle chatter. And while he was often the subject of gossip and careless of it—he recognised that a quick coupling with the stable girl might be going just a little too far. He was reckless, yes—but he was not completely stupid.

He loosened his grip slightly—not letting her go completely because he realised that she might actually faint. A woman fainting in his arms—yet another of his fantasies come true! For a moment a passion so sweet and so intensely powerful coursed through his veins that his resolve was severely tested.

But surely it would be much *easier* to have his way with her in Europe—where sexual freedom was taken for granted? He could enjoy her sweet, virginal body—and give her the heady experience he had promised. No one would know—even if they did, who would particularly care? And afterwards he could dismiss her and make sure that she was set up for life. She would have memories of bliss to keep her warm during the long, harsh nights of winter.

'Don't worry your pretty little head about it, lizard,' he drawled.

Eleni looked up at him and bit her bottom lip. 'Why do you call me lizard?'

His mouth curved. 'Because your eyes are so green and you move almost without seeming to and with such supple grace.' He lifted his hand and cupped her chin in his palm. 'And because you are very quick.'

There was a breathless moment where he could see her face glow—clearly flattered at the nickname—and so she should be. *Take her* now, he thought urgently, and then he looked up to see Abdul-Aziz walking across the stable yard towards them and abruptly Kaliq let Eleni go with an impatient sigh.

It was the first time he had seen his aide since he'd returned from the neighbouring island of Aristo, where he had represented Kaliq at the funeral of King Aegeus.

'So how goes the great fight for the succession of the dead king?' asked Kaliq, even though in his heart he did not care—for the rivalries between the two royal families of

Calista and Aristo had tainted the history of the two islands for many long years.

Abdul-Aziz's gaze flickered uncertainly to Eleni, who was still standing there, waiting to be dismissed.

'Do not worry, she is loyal,' said Kaliq and Eleni hated herself for the fierce feeling of pleasure which those simple words of praise produced.

Abdul-Aziz gave a bow. 'The succession is by no means certain, Highness.'

'Prince Sebastian is eager to inherit, is he not?' mocked Kaliq. 'Ah, but ambition makes such vultures of men. How happy I am not to have dynastic ambition ruling *my* life!'

'Indeed, Highness,' said Abdul-Aziz, with another small bow. 'Would you care to hear a report of how the day went?'

'You think that I am interested in all the family feuding?' Kaliq murmured, but Abdul-Aziz was looking especially solemn and so he made an impatient gesture with his hand. 'Oh, very well, let us return to the palace and you can tell me all about it.' He shot a quick glance at Eleni. 'Oh, and by the way, Aziz—my new stable girl is to accompany me to England to look at that polo horse I was telling you about.'

Abdul-Aziz started. 'Accompany you?'

'That's what I said,' drawled Kaliq.

'But, Highness—'

Black eyes pierced through the aide like twin ebony swords. 'But *what*, Aziz?' he echoed silkily. 'You think that tongues will wag?'

'Well, yes, Highness.'

'Then let them—because only the tails of dogs and horses are meant for wagging! And I am taking the girl with me—that is the beginning and the end of the matter. We will leave by jet in the morning, do you understand?'

His face impassive, Abdul-Aziz nodded with the resignation of one who had spent their life taking orders from resolute rulers and Eleni found herself wondering how he could bear never to be able to answer back. 'Yes, Highness.'

'Good. Then please arrange it.'

And, giving Eleni one last mocking look, Kaliq swept from the stable yard, leaving her staring after him with a fast-beating heart and a mass of mixed emotions.

CHAPTER EIGHT

'You can let go of my hand now,' said Kaliq softly. 'And open up your eyes, lizard—for nothing is going to happen to you.'

Eleni hadn't even noticed she'd been gripping the sheikh's hand! Tentatively, she loosened her grip as she allowed her eyelids to flutter open to see his dark and mocking face uncomfortably yet tantalisingly close to hers as he sat beside her on the luxury jet. And once again she willed away the feeling of fear as she allowed her gaze to flicker to the round windows of the plane. 'I am flying through the air,' she croaked in disbelief.

'Oh, please don't come over with all that ancient witchcraft stuff with me,' he mocked.

'You must have seen planes passing over Calista countless times.'

'But I have never travelled on one before, Highness—nor ever imagined that I would.'

'Your first time,' he mused softly. 'How exciting that must be.'

'Exciting?' Eleni quaked—not caring whether she was meant to answer his observation because she was still shaking from the experience of being whisked through the palm-tree lined streets of Jaladhar in a 'four-wheel drive' to the airport. A big beast of a car which had been light years away from the battered old rusty wreck owned by her father. 'Terrifying would be a more accurate description,' she answered truthfully.

'Such an attitude does not bode well for any future new experiences, lizard,' he murmured—though his mind was preoccupied with only one. For the greatest experience of all awaited her later in his arms. He studied her, thinking how very provincial she looked with those braids of hair which fell to her slender waist. How would she cope in England? he wondered. 'Have you never wanted your own car?' he questioned curiously.

'Certainly not,' Eleni returned. 'They have but limited use in the desert regions—a horse is quicker across the sands and more reliable, too, and the car makes people lazy.'

'Oh, does it?' Kaliq's eyes glinted. 'Are you accusing me of being lazy?'

Eleni briefly let her eyelids fall. 'I do not know enough about to you to pronounce such a judgement, Highness—even if I dared to break protocol by doing so.'

He studied her thoughtfully. 'Sometimes I almost think that you are being sardonic, lizard—until I remember that a desert girl would know little of such subtlety.'

Eleni couldn't help herself. Was it the unreal experience of being lifted into the clouds which had tipped all the normal rules of life upside down? Why else would she have dared to consider answering the sheikh in such a way? Surely not because she had known what it was like to be held and kissed by him?

'You told me that western women would patronise me because of the way I look,' she said. 'And yet you now do the same. You speak of subtlety and tell me that I can have no understanding of it—yet why shouldn't I? For it is just a variation on human behaviour and I am human—just the same as you.'

Kaliq frowned, and yet he accepted that she had a valid point—it was just that she was the last person on earth he would have expected to make such a point. 'It was not intended as a criticism,' he said, in a voice which was as close as he ever got to gentle. 'More an ob-servation. But you seem almost—educated—for one from such a background as yours.'

'But I *am* educated, Highness. You see, I—' And then she stopped abruptly. What in the falcon's name was she doing talking to the sheikh about matters such as this? Her tongue had run away with her. 'Forgive me,' she mumbled. 'I forget myself.'

'No, no.' He shook his dark head. 'Your remarks interest me, Eleni. You give me insight into the lives of my subjects. Pray, continue.'

Eleni wriggled her shoulders a little. 'Well, I *liked* school. The educational reforms initiated by your stepmother, Queen Anya, meant that girls like me were given access to books and learning for the first time. I had a teacher who encouraged me—she let me read her own books—novels,' she elaborated shyly.

It had been like a sweet, long draft of water after a hot ride in the desert to sit at a desk and be given clean white paper and pens. An escape from the drudgery at home and the tyrannical reign of her father.

'So why did you leave school if you liked it so much?' he questioned softly. 'You could have gone on to further study—it is rarer among girls, it is true, but the opportunities are there, and Jaladhar has its own university.'

Eleni stared at him. 'Because I was poor,' she said, her cheeks flushing pink.

'There are scholarships, Eleni,' he pointed out.

'And because my father would never have allowed it. Because ultimately, men still make the decisions in Calista and women obey them, no matter how great the opportunities which lie before them.'

Kaliq was silent for a moment. She was turning out to be much cleverer than he had ever anticipated—with a native cunning which could spell trouble if he was not careful. She was here simply to help him decide on a horse and to warm his bed at night—and neither of them should forget that. So whose fault was it that they now seemed to be steering towards an inappropriate debate on the openings available for women in Calista? His!

'Make yourself ready—for we are about to land. It can be a startling experience—but there is nothing for you to fear,' he said coolly, and began to flick through an English newspaper, knowing that his words weren't quite true. But what purpose would there be in telling her that take-off and landing were the two most dangerous moments during a flight?

Eleni wondered what had happened to make his attitude change so suddenly—but then the engines began to make a huge sound like the roaring of a thousand thunderstorms and she was too preoccupied to care.

And when she had shakily made her way down the aircraft steps, a big shiny black car was waiting to whisk them through narrow little roads which Kaliq called 'lanes' and which were lined with the thickest and greenest hedges that Eleni had ever seen. It all looked so lush and so beautiful that some of her trepidation dissolved. What had her teacher at school told her? That life was there to be experienced and enjoyed. So what was the point of worrying about what *might* happen? It hadn't happened yet.

'You like what you see?' he queried as he heard her soft sigh.

She turned to him, her eyes were shining. 'Oh, yes, Highness!'

'We are going to my house in Surrey,' he said, wondering if she knew just how potent that kind of unfeigned enthusiasm could be. No, of course not. She was a simple girl from the country—and a virgin—so what would she know of men's desires? 'I thought that you might find London a little overwhelming—and this is much closer to the stables we are going to visit.'

'You…you *own* a house in England?' Eleni questioned uncertainly.

'I do.'

'So you mean, this is where you live when you are not in Calista?'

'Oh, I stay here when I'm in England and feel a hankering for the countryside,' he said dismissively. 'But I also keep a place in New York, an apartment in Milan and a villa in the South of France.'

'So many homes!'

Her tone seemed to imply puzzlement rather than admiration and Kaliq's mouth twisted into an odd kind of smile. At least nobody could ever accuse her of being a gold-digger! 'Staying in hotels is beset with difficulties,' he explained, without stopping to ask himself why he was bothering to offer his stable girl some kind of explanation for his conduct. 'It means I have to rely on someone else's security arrangements.'

'Oh, I see,' said Eleni slowly, remembering that time at her father's when he had made her taste his pomegranate juice first, in case it was poisoned. When he was talking to her like this it was almost foolishly easy to forget that he was a prince—and to some, perhaps, a target. 'But I do not notice any bodyguards, Highness.'

'There is a car ahead of us and one behind—but they are discreet because that is how I like it. And sometimes I prefer not to have any at all…when their presence would *inhibit* me,' he added, with a glitter in his black eyes which Eleni did not understand. 'But my estate here is so well guarded that I have a certain kind of freedom when I am here. Now look over there,' he instructed softly. 'For we have arrived.'

Nothing could have prepared Eleni for that first sight of the sheikh's English home. His palace in Calista was splendid—so lavish and rich and sumptuous—but this was different and so totally outside her experience that for a moment it completely overwhelmed her.

'Oh!' she exclaimed, her fingers fluttering to her lips as she stared in disbelief.

'What do you think of it?'

The house rose up from a lawn of impossible greenness—a stately building of bricks as warm and as red as a desert sunset. There were stone steps leading up to a huge door flanked by carved pillars. And everywhere she looked, she could see flowers dancing—they had frilly trumpets and were coloured saffron.

'It's…it is beautiful, Highness. Truly beautiful.'

Ridiculously, her comment pleased him—for he sensed it came from the heart rather than because it would be what he was expecting to hear. And for a man who spent his life having his moods gauged and his wishes judged it was as refreshing as the summer rain. 'Why, thank you,' he said gravely.

'And look at the flowers—I have never seen quite so many in one place!'

'Daffodils,' he said unsteadily, thinking that the colour of her eyes was as green as the fresh young growth of spring. 'They are called daffodils. There's a very famous poem written about them by a man named Wordsworth.'

'I should like to read it,' Eleni said wistfully.

'You shall.' And suddenly, he couldn't stop himself. The moist gleam of her mouth was too provocative and her innocent sense of wonder was like an unexpectedly powerful aphrodisiac—and Kaliq leaned over, pulling her into his arms. He looked down at her. 'You shall do many things when you are with me, Eleni—do you understand that?'

Staring up into his face, she saw a look of intent written in the glitter of his eyes and Eleni knew what was about to happen. But it was not fear she felt in her heart but a great sense of longing. There was a split second when she tried to tell herself this was wrong—but the sight of his hard, dark features dominating her vision wiped away the nagging voice of doubt on Eleni's lips.

Because she was impatient for his kiss—greedy to taste it once more. It was as if the sheikh had woken in her a dormant hunger she hadn't known existed until he had liberated it with the first touch of his lips back in Calista.

'*Oh,*' she breathed as his lips began to explore hers with a thoroughness which took her breath away.

Kaliq kissed her and, to his astonishment,

she kissed him back as sweetly as the most experienced lover. Kissed him until there was no breath left in his lungs and he levered himself away from her to gaze down into the wide-eyed wonder of her face. 'It's good, isn't it, lizard?' he questioned unevenly. 'To kiss like this?'

Eleni swallowed. 'Oh, *yes*, Highness.'

Quickly, he claimed her mouth once more—enjoying her little whimper of pleasure as he took control. She was like an unbroken horse, he realised. All fire and spirit—with an innate need to be conquered. And how quickly she learned, he thought with admiration—as her hands reached up to softly knead at his shoulders and he imagined those fingers pressing into his naked flesh.

He felt the moist softness of her lips—the shy and darting uncertainty of her tongue as it mimicked the movement of his and flicked inside his mouth. Hesitantly, at first—and then with a growing confidence until it became a lazy curl against the roof of his mouth which made him groan.

He pushed her back against the soft leather seat and he could see that the amazing pistachio-green of her eyes had almost completely been obscured by the dark brilliance of desire. Her firm, young breasts were pushing against the silk of the tunic she was wearing—their pert tips as hard as Calistan diamonds—and how he longed to bare them. To feast his eyes on her naked flesh. To take them into his mouth and suckle them.

He pushed back the hair from her flushed face, sensing that sexual desire had her firmly in its grip. Knowing that he could slide the silk from her body and explore her secret places which no man had ever touched. Why, no doubt he could loosen the cord of his silk trousers and impale her here, on the back seat of the car—until she cried out with her pleasure.

His gaze flicked to the tinted window of the limousine—but already he could see activity beginning. The staff had been alerted and told that their sheikh was here. And now he found himself looking at Eleni as if through new eyes—seeing her as an outsider might see her.

His closest aides were from Calista, yes—but some of the resident staff here were English. How would it look if he emerged from the car bearing the wild-haired stable girl with seduction having just taken place on the back seat of the car?

He frowned. Eleni had natural skills and talents with a horse which most of them would only ever dream of—but how could she possibly assert any kind of authority here if she was seen as his submissive lover? The kind of woman who would simply let a man take her in a semi-public place?

Angry with his own thoughts and where they were taking him, Kaliq moved away from her—trying to quell the fierce throb of desire which pulsed at his groin.

What the hell was the matter with him?

'Tidy your hair!' he snapped. 'And make yourself presentable to meet my staff.'

Eleni quickly sat up and smoothed her hands over her tousled braids, horribly aware of the position she had put herself in by allowing herself to be so easily seduced. Her heart was still thumping and her cheeks felt as if they were on fire—why, if the sheikh had not stopped what he was doing there was no saying *what* might now be happening.

You know exactly what would be happening, Eleni—taunted the mocking voice of her conscience.

Her colour increased as the sheikh tapped at the dark glass interconnecting panel between driver and passenger—and this must have set off some smooth mechanism, for almost immediately a shadow loomed up outside the car window, and the door was opened by a member of staff.

It was a woman—quite obviously a Calistan national judging by her dark eyes and golden-olive skin. But she was dressed in a way that Eleni had never seen before. She wore a slim-fitting skirt which came to just below her knees—and a pair of soft leather boots which looked almost like riding boots! Tucked into the waistband of the skirt was a beautiful soft white blouse and the woman wore her dark hair loose—it hung down to her shoulders in a manner which suggested that she might regularly cut it. Why, she was dressed like a westerner! Eleni blinked as the woman gave a smooth curtsey to the sheikh.

'This is Zahra,' drawled Kaliq. 'She helps run my office for me in England. She will arrange everything you need. Put Eleni in the white room, Zahra,' he added, and swept past them—his mouth hard with displeasure. 'I am going to my office.'

Eleni watched him go, suddenly fearful. Her heart was still beating hard from that passionate encounter and, shamefully, her body was aching—but watching the sheikh walk away, leaving her alone with this rather glamorous stranger, made Eleni feel suddenly alone, and adrift.

'How was your flight?' asked Zahra—her voice breaking into Eleni's troubled thoughts.

Eleni hesitated. Did royal protocol mean that she should say it was wonderful? That the prince's flight was both luxurious and comfortable—because that much was true. But too many experiences had been packed into such a short space of time for her to be able to maintain any kind of façade. And why pretend to be something she wasn't? 'I was terrified,' she admitted. 'It was the first time I had ever been on a plane!'

Zahra bit back a smile. 'Ah, yes, I remember the feeling well. The first time I flew from Calista, I felt as if it were happening to someone else. But you are here safely now—so shall I show you to your suite and you can freshen up and change?'

Eleni nodded, her spirits lifted by the

thought of having another bath. It was funny how quickly she had become used to the luxury of running water. 'Yes, please.'

Inside, the entrance hall was so big that it contained a huge fireplace, piled with logs and ready to be lit. And the wooden staircase was just as impressive—carved with leaves and flowers as it swept upwards. Eleni stood for a moment just looking at it.

'By the raven's wing,' she murmured. 'This is indeed a beautiful place.'

'Indeed it is.' Zahra glanced at her as she indicated for Eleni to follow her upstairs. 'The Sheikh Kaliq Al'Farisi tells me that you are a great horsewoman.'

Eleni smiled. 'The sheikh is indeed very gracious.'

'And his office tells me that you will require English clothes.'

Eleni glanced at Zahra's neat dark skirt and the soft white blouse. The other Calistan woman looked perfectly...*decent*, did she not? Yet Eleni hesitated as she remembered the way that Kaliq's jodhpurs had hugged every inch of his hips and bottom, and she shook her head. How could she possibly go out dressed in such a way?

'I do not wish to reject the values of my country,' she said fiercely—and the subject was temporarily forgotten as Zahra opened the door and showed her into a room of breathtaking simplicity.

Everything was white—snowy white like the peaks of winter mountains. There were white walls and a thick white carpet which sank beneath her feet like quicksand. Muslin drapes like drifts of clouds hung from a large four-poster bed covered in dazzling white linen and beautiful embroidered white curtains framed a picture-perfect view from the huge windows.

'This is your room.' Zahra smiled.

Eleni smiled back, her heart suddenly light. *He really does treat his staff well*, she thought as she peered through an open door to see a pristine white bathroom of majestic proportions. As she turned to speak to Zahra she saw another door which she hadn't previously noticed.

'And where does that one lead to?' she questioned innocently.

'That one?' Zahra's face remained impassive. 'Oh, that door connects you to the suite of the sheikh.'

CHAPTER NINE

ELENI was in a terrible dilemma as she dressed for dinner, defiantly picking out the most traditional outfit from the batch she had brought with her from the sheikh's palace in Calista. And all the time, a single question buzzed round and round in her head like a fly mesmerised by a candle flame.

Had the prince *deliberately* put her into a suite with a door which connected to his—and was he planning to *use* it?

But surely it would be impertinent to ask him—as if she was questioning his motives. Even perhaps a little *presumptuous*—almost as if she was *expecting* him to try to enter her room?

And aren't you? taunted that rogue voice in her head which kept stirring up uncomfortable thoughts and feelings no matter how hard she tried to quell it. Hadn't she thought of little else other than the way his lips had felt as he had pushed her down onto the back seat of the car and…and…

Cheeks stinging, she finished tying back her hair before going over to the door in question to check whether or not there was a key. And why did she register no surprise whatsoever to discover that there *wasn't* one?

Her hands were trembling as she heard a tap at the door and there was Zahra, waiting to lead her down to dinner.

'I thought I'd come and get you myself,' she said kindly. 'Rather than send one of the servants.'

And as Eleni followed her down the sweeping staircase she made up her mind that if the sheikh came to her in the night, she would simply tell him no. Because although he was a man—and a highly virile man at his peak—she knew deep down that he would never take her by force.

But Kaliq seemed preoccupied throughout the meal, his brow furrowed deep by a frown. He kept getting called out by Zahra to take telephone calls, leaving Eleni sitting there rather self-consciously on her own while a stream of servants glided through offering her golden dishes of titbits she had no appetite for.

She was just wondering whether she could slip away unnoticed when he returned, his eyes narrowing as she sat there with a half-eaten pear in front of her—as if he had only just noticed her for the first time. He sat down opposite her, and sighed.

'I have been a bad host tonight, lizard—forgive me.'

'It is not the sheikh's place to seek the forgiveness of one of his subjects,' answered Eleni dutifully, hoping that a little protocol might emphasise all the differences between them.

'How very prim and proper you sound this evening,' he murmured sardonically. 'Few would guess that you had been lying in my arms just a few hours earlier—with your body craving more of my touch!'

'Highness!' Eleni whispered, appalled—but he shrugged his shoulders.

'*Highness*, what?' he mocked. 'Highness, don't tell the truth? Don't you like the truth, Eleni? Or are you trying to pretend that if I hadn't called a halt to your sweet submissiveness, then I should have taken your virginity in the back of my limousine?'

Once again, her cheeks were on fire, but so too—more worryingly—was her body. A strange aching had made her breasts feel so heavy—just like that peculiar sensation she'd first experienced in the scented bathwater at Kaliq's palace. This was desire, Eleni realised—and the sheikh was such a proficient lover that he could manufacture it by words which were not even sweet or admiring!

'No?' he continued ruthlessly. 'Nothing to say?'

She could sense the unknown and potent danger in the air. His eyes were challenging and his body language was suddenly tense and Eleni recognised that if she allowed this conversation to continue, then it might end up in the place she most wanted yet most feared to be. In his arms.

'I am very tired after the journey and I would ask the sheikh if I may be excused,' said Eleni stiffly.

There was a pause as Kaliq's eyes narrowed. *Excessively* formal, he thought. And how insolent of her to ask to be excused before her royal host had left the room. But mightn't it be easier to have her stripped naked and waiting for him?

'Then don't let me stop you,' he drawled. 'In fact, I have business I need to deal with.' His black eyes glittered with anticipation. 'Think you can find your way back upstairs?'

'Of course,' said Eleni, the heavy chair scraping back as she stood up, her heart beating fast beneath her breast. Remind him why you're here—and remind yourself in the process before you get carried away with this rich and privileged life of his. 'And when will we see the horse?'

'Tomorrow. There is a polo match at a nearby ground—you might as well see him in action before you exercise your judgement.'

'I shall look forward to that.' Eleni curt-seyed. 'Good…goodnight, Highness.'

His lips curved into a sardonic smile as he heard her tremulous hesitation. She was innocent, yes—but she had a natural intelligence which surely would not deny the chemistry which existed between them. Did she really think that she would lie alone tonight? That he would allow that to happen?

'Goodnight, Eleni.'

Her mouth dry with nameless fear, Eleni went upstairs to her room—trying to tell herself that of course she wasn't surprised or disappointed that the sheikh had let her go so easily. For hadn't his words unsettled her? The way he had described her response to him in the back of the car—why, it had made her feel ashamed and yet full of desire, all at the same time!

But it was with a sense of urgency that she undressed quickly—her hair still ribboned as she turned off all the lights and then slipped between the sheets.

Through the filmy curtains was a silver scythe curve of moon and she could see the occasional pinprick of a star—but they looked like pale imitations of the bright stars in the Calistan heavens, and suddenly Eleni felt very alone.

She tried to keep awake, to be on her guard in case the arrogant prince tried to enter her bedroom uninvited. And she should have been too excited and nervous to sleep after everything that had happened—the drive, the flight, the fact that she, Eleni Lakis, was in *England*! But one way or another it had been an exhausting day and the bed was unbelievably comfortable so that she couldn't seem to stop eyelids which felt as if they had been weighted by lead, from shutting out the world.

It seemed like only seconds later that Eleni awoke to the sensation of the bed dipping and her eyes snapped open in alarm. For a moment then it had almost felt as if someone was... *getting into bed beside her*!

Her eyes adjusting to the half-light from the stars outside, she turned her head and there... there...lying next to her as if he had every right to be there and *clearly naked as the day he had first entered the world of men*—was the Sheikh Kaliq Al'Farisi!

She sat bolt upright in bed, her fingertips flying to her throat, feeling the pulse fluttering wildly beneath. 'By the desert storm,' she breathed. 'What do you think you're doing here?'

He gave a soft laugh as he reached his hand up to twist a silken braid of hair around his fingers. 'Innocent you might be, my beauty—but I don't really think you need me to give you an answer to that, do you, Eleni?'

Afterwards, she told herself that she might have screamed—had he not pulled her down against his bare flesh. And the sensations which powered over her were so intense that she closed her eyes and prayed that she would be strong in the path of such temptation.

'Highness, *please*!' she protested.

'Please, what? Please this…?'

Almost lazily, he drifted his lips to hers and kissed her, feeling her tremble beneath his touch.

'H-Highness!' she stumbled, weakly.

Kaliq levered himself up to look down into her face, his expression stern—his eyes glittering fiercely in the half-light as they raked over her with proprietorial hunger.

'Now listen to me while I tell you this and listen well. For tonight I am not your Highness, Eleni,' he said. 'Tonight I am just

Kaliq. In this bed at least, we are equals. Do you understand that?'

And a little bit of Eleni's heart turned over as she heard the simple appeal in his words— the sense that tonight he just wanted to be treated as a man and not a prince. Could she deny him a gift so simple—or was that just wishful thinking on her part?

She wanted to ask him how he thought that she could ever call him by his Christian name—but by then the sheikh's hand had moved beneath the sheet and had taken her breast. It seemed that he, at least, had no problem with familiarity. Eleni closed her eyes, trying to fight the great wave of pleasure which whispered through her as he cupped the small globe and teased its tip into throbbing life.

'H-Highness!' she gasped.

'Kaliq!' he reminded her.

'K-Kaliq!' Vaguely, she thought how odd it was to utter the name of her sheikh—and yet

how delicious it felt on her lips. Nearly as delicious as the sweet caress of his fingers.

'Yes, Eleni, what is it?'

'I…I…' She shook her braided hair distract-
edly against the pillow as he worked some kind
of magic with his touch. *I don't remember.*

In the semi-darkness, he smiled as he continued to stroke her. 'That's good. Just feel.
Just enjoy what I'm doing to you. Tell me, do
you like it when I do that, Eleni?'

'Oh! Oh. *Oh!*'

'I think we must judge from your response
that you do,' he murmured drily. 'Shall we try
something else?'

Carelessly, he let his fingertips trail to dip
into her belly button and let them stay there—
waiting instinctively until she circled her hips
in restless but silent entreaty. And then
slowly—more slowly than he had ever moved
in his life—he moved his hand lower still until
he had delved deep into her honeyed sweetness—and was taken aback by how fresh and

how ready she was for him. 'And what about here—do you like me touching you here, too?'

As she bucked beneath his fingers Eleni honestly thought she was going to faint with pleasure—that was if she allowed herself to give into it, and not focus on the fact that this was the *sheikh*. Or just what he was doing to her. 'But surely that is *wrong*?' she breathed as he moved luxuriantly against her heated flesh.

Kaliq swallowed, strangely moved by her combination of innocence and enthusiasm. 'How can it be wrong when it is what a man and a woman were designed for?' he questioned huskily.

Eleni felt as if she were drowning in unbelievable sweetness—far sweeter than anything she had ever known. She knew the basics of sex— of course she did—so why was the sheikh not joining with her as she expected him to?

Why was he moving his fingers deliciously between her legs like that—making her feel as if control was slipping away? As if a place of undreamed-of delight were beckoning to her and she were sliding towards it. Eleni began to tremble and tears began to blur her eyes as waves of ecstasy began to shudder through her.

'K-Kaliq!' she gasped.

He almost lit the lamp to watch her very first orgasm but he did not want to destroy the mood. As it was, the half-light caught her joy and illuminated the tear which trickled slowly down over her cheek and he lowered his head to lick it away.

'Do not cry,' he said softly and then, inexplicably, he felt a sudden lurching of his heart. 'Are you sad that I took your purity away?'

Eleni shook her head, and laid it on his chest, where she could feel the beat of his lifeblood as it pulsed through him. 'How could I be sad about something which was so beautiful?' she whispered, her voice still dazed. 'Why, to feel that way seems scarcely human.'

'That is why some say the act of love is

divine,' he murmured. 'Now come here, and I will show you more beauty still.'

Moving over her, he stroked a few wisps of tangled curls away from her face and she wrapped her arms around his neck, looking up at him with utter trust. What a straightforward lover she was proving to be, he thought—as honest and as fearless as she was in the saddle!

His lips grazed over hers—at first almost lazily—as if he were coaxing from them another trembling response. And then the kiss deepened and became more intense—and suddenly he could wait no longer.

Parting her firm thighs, he thrust into her with one long stroke as he heard her stifle the cry as her innocence was taken from her for ever. How hot and tight she felt. Kaliq moaned. He could have spilled his seed into her right there and then—and why not? For it was the right of the sheikh to take his pleasure where he found it.

Yet strangely he found himself wanting this

eager, unexpected beauty to have the time of her life. To gasp her pleasure once more beneath the onslaught of his sexual prowess. So he held back. He tantalised her with the thrust of his body and then retreated, over and over again until the body of his no-longer-a-virgin began to adjust and to acclimatise to the new sensations which were sweeping over her. How quickly she learnt, he thought in admiration as he sensed her pleasure building once more.

'Kaliq!' she whispered.

In the darkness, he smiled. And how quickly she had adjusted to the familiar use of his name, too! 'What is it, my green-eyed lovely?'

'It's…it's… *Oh*! That thing…that *thing*… it's going to *happen all over again*!'

'Your orgasm,' he purred—but this time as she convulsed around his aching flesh he joined her, letting go completely, losing himself in a sea of delight, his body juddering as it was racked with spasms which seemed to go on and on, leaving him completely dry and gasping.

Afterwards he lay back against the heap of pillows, staring rather dazedly up at the ceiling—knowing that he should now go back to his own suite and yet strangely reluctant to do so. She was snuggling up to him, wrapping her warm body around his, and he was usually irritated by such cloying familiarity once the sexual act had been completed. But with Eleni he felt no such irritation.

Was that because he was safe from ambition with her? That such a lowly lover as her would simply be grateful for whatever he gave her and would not dare to make the demands of the majority of her sex?

He would just close his eyes for a moment and then he would go back to his suite….

Beside him, Eleni lay listening to his steady breathing as he slipped into sleep, while the facts of what had just happened began to sink into her glowing body. Truly, she was no longer a girl—she had been made into a woman by her sheikh.

Carefully, she turned her head to look at him. His dark hair was tousled and as he slept his harsh features were relaxed. How bizarre to think that the Prince of Calista lay naked beside her. That his body had been intimately joined with hers—just as she had seen the stallions rutting the mares in the stable.

But this was different. Horses did not have emotions that felt as if a great big bit of mountain had just fallen down on top of you. She bit her lip. And what did this extraordinary night mean? Were they to become lovers, or would Kaliq simply cast her off in the morning and pretend that nothing had happened?

So troubled were Eleni's thoughts that she should not have slept, but she *did* sleep—a fact she only discovered by being woken by the soft touch of a fingertip over each of her eyelids.

Her eyes fluttered open to find that the early morning sun was creeping in through the muslin drapes and that Kaliq was looking down at her. Anxiously, she searched his face for a sign of what last night had meant to *him*. Did he still respect her? Consider her to be a worthy lover? But the ebony eyes were as hard as chips of bright ebony and his sensual lips gave nothing away, except—she thought, with the beginnings of experience—a sense that they would like to kiss her again.

'So what did you think of your sexual awakening, lizard?'

She felt the colour stealing into her cheeks. What was she expected to say? 'It was very…agreeable.'

'Agreeable?' He laughed softly, thinking how ironic it was that his little stable girl should give him such a cool response—he, who had been praised to the heavens by society beauties the world over. 'Agreeable enough to want to do it again?' he mocked as he touched the outline of her lips with his finger.

His flesh contained the scent of something sultry and soapy—something that Eleni knew was connected to her and she felt the colour flaming to her cheeks once more. And there was no place to hide in the cruel light of day. 'Highness…Kaliq…I…'

Kaliq frowned. Last night, in the passion and heat of the moment, he had overlooked the fact that she was not just inexperienced physically—but emotionally, too. And this morning he needed to make the situation clear to her—because he could not afford for her to misread it.

'Before we continue, there is something I must tell you, Eleni,' he said softly, tilting her chin upwards so that she was forced to look at him. 'You know that sex is always different for a woman?'

She stared at him in confusion.

'Some women do not have the same capacity as a man to enjoy the act—or so I believe,' he added truthfully, 'since no woman in my bed has ever experienced anything but pleasure.' He ignored her wince of pain—but he had merely been stating a fact. Was she foolishly allowing herself the fantasy of thinking that *he* had never known any other lover than her?

'Nature has designed a man and a woman differently,' he continued firmly. 'For men sex is simply the natural spilling of their seed, but for women it is merely the trigger—and deep down they are searching for a mate to father their children. That is what makes women start attaching emotion to the act.'

'E-emotion?' Eleni felt as if he was insulting her—she just wasn't quite sure how, or why? 'I don't understand what you mean.'

He steeled himself against the naked pain in her face. 'I mean that women sometimes convince themselves that they're falling in love with a man once they've had sex with him—because it seems to make the act more respectable in their eyes.'

For a moment, Eleni didn't react until the full impact of his words hit her. Of all the cold-hearted and cruel men she could have picked as her lover—then Kaliq must be the very worst. She tried to tell herself that she could have resisted him. *Should* have resisted him—but she knew that was a lie. She could have no more resisted the sheikh than a man crawling in the desert for three days could have resisted a cool, clear flagon of fresh water. She had had no control over her reaction to him—physically, at least.

But she saw now that she needed to protect herself as much as possible against the inevitable pain which would follow if she did not heed his words. If she were foolish enough to fall in love with a man who would toss her aside in an instant if he needed to.

No, she would learn everything she could from her royal lover—would study sexual techniques in the same way that she had learned about horses. She would become an expert lover in his bed…and when the affair was concluded, she would leave the arrogant and dismissive sheikh aching for her.

'I agree completely, Kaliq,' she agreed imperturbably.

His eyes narrowed. 'You do?'

'But of course. And you need have no concerns about me. For why would I waste my time falling in love with a man with whom there was no earthly possibility of a future?'

This should have been the perfect answer—but to Kaliq's fury, it made him feel utterly indignant. Why, she had accepted her fate without shedding even a single tear! Did she think that she would find him easy to forget? Well, she would soon learn how wrong she had been.

Kaliq moved his hand beneath the sheet. 'I am bored with talking,' he growled as he guided her fingers to his aching flesh. 'Come here and kiss me.'

And even as Eleni obeyed—the pleasure happening all over again as he thrust into her—she remained glad that she had sounded both proud and independent. But if this was victory—then it must have been the most short-lived in the history of the world. Because after he had made love to her with an almost ruthless efficiency which left her gasping, he got out of bed—seeming to enjoy her blushes as he paraded his magnificent nakedness against the stark backdrop of the snowy room.

'We will leave for the polo match after lunch,' he said.

Eleni pulled the sheet up to her chin and nodded. 'Yes, Kaliq.'

Pausing in the act of knotting the belt of his robe, he flicked her an impenetrable look. 'Just two things,' he drawled. 'When you prepare for bed tonight, don't braid your hair like a governess—I wish to see it spread loose over my pillow.'

Her fingers playing with one of the ribbons, Eleni looked at him, unable to deny the small spring of hope in her heart. 'And the other?'

His smile was cruel. 'Make sure you don't ever call me Kaliq in public.'

CHAPTER TEN

'COFFEE, Eleni?'

Eleni sat down at the breakfast table as Zahra held up a heavy silver pot, wondering if her face or her demeanour gave the sheikh's assistant any hint of what had happened last night.

Or was this a house with no secrets—the interconnecting door of her bedroom giving the game away to all? Did the servants realise that, under cover of darkness, Prince Kaliq had crept into the bed of his stable girl and taken her virginity in the most heartbreakingly beautiful way possible? Why, maybe Zahra herself had gone through a similar initiation ceremony.

Eleni's cheeks flamed and she felt her heart

give a painful lurch. *Please let that not be the case*, she prayed silently. 'I'd love some coffee,' she said quietly.

Zahra upended some inky brew into a tiny golden coffee cup and pushed it across the table. 'The sheikh has asked me to tell you that someone will be over after breakfast. You can be measured up and a selection of outfits sent over within the hour. Something for you to wear to the polo match.' Zahra smiled. 'It'll be fun—believe me.'

But Eleni was still smarting from Kaliq's command that she never call him by his given name in public. And while she knew that his words made sense, it didn't stop them hurting—but at least it helped her come to a decision. He had set out *his* rules very firmly—so why should she not have rules of her own? Why should she dress up to be something she wasn't? Masquerading as a cute western mannequin until Kaliq tired of her and it was time to put her back into the cupboard?

And besides—she already felt displaced enough in this English home of the sheikh's. Surely if she started dressing like a westerner then she would end up feeling completely alienated?

'Please thank the sheikh for his generous offer,' she said stiffly. 'But also tell him that I cannot accept it. There is no reason why I should not go to the polo match dressed in traditional gown. I am there to assess a horse and not to impress others.'

Zahra gave her an uneasy smile as she offered a basket of warm bread. 'I'll tell him,' she said. 'But I can tell you now, Eleni—he won't like it.'

Eleni shrugged. No, she could imagine that Kaliq was a man who never liked being disobeyed in anything. 'Where *is* the sheikh this morning?' asked Eleni, telling herself that Zahra's slightly ominous words were not going to frighten her.

'He's in his office.' Zahra hesitated for a moment. 'Do you need to speak to him?'

Too quickly, Eleni shook her head. 'No. I have no wish to disturb him.'

She needed to get out into the fresh air. To cool down her overheated body and blow her disquiet away, and after coffee she went out to explore the grounds—discovering a small wood carpeted with blue flowers shaped like bells.

Her mood kept veering wildly between dreamy recollections of what had happened to her last night. Of her first initiation into the act of love with a man who could not have been a more perfect lover. Except that there was no love involved, she reminded herself bitterly. No feeling at all, it seemed. The sheikh had made *that* very clear indeed—illustrated by the way he had described sex in such a mechanical and unfeeling way! Did he not care how cruel and cold he had been to a woman who had welcomed him into her body during that blissful night?

She picked one of the blue flowers and held it to her nose, inhaling its sweet scent. Of course he didn't. She was his *servant*, wasn't she? His stable girl—nothing more than that. And she never would be.

Just before they left for the polo match, Eleni showered and changed into silk tunic and trousers and Kaliq's eyes narrowed when he walked into the room and saw her.

So she had ignored his instructions, he thought grimly. He had been looking forward to seeing that superb, tight bottom encased in a clinging pair of jodhpurs. Or a sleek and fitted dress.

'You will stand out by a mile, dressed like that,' he offered drily. 'And yet Zahra tells me you turned down the clothes which were offered to you.'

'Indeed I did.'

'Stubborn, obstinate Eleni,' he said, in a low voice. 'And why did you do that?'

'Because I would rather be true to myself than pretend to be something I'm not, Highness,' she replied as she bobbed him a curtsey.

He glanced at her—cursing the folds of silk which concealed her slender body from his eyes. How dared she have the temerity to disobey his wishes and cover herself up?

'No coy look for your prince this morning?' he mocked. 'No murmured thanks for the treasures he brought to your bed-chamber last night which made you gasp aloud with such joy?'

Eleni kept her face expressionless, even though inside her heart was racing so fast that she felt dizzy. 'But you told me not to be familiar with you in public, Highness,' she protested.

He glanced around. 'And you can see for yourself that the room is empty!'

Her smile was serene. 'Far better to get into practice of maintaining normal protocol, Highness—that way no embarrassing mistakes can be made.'

To his fury, Kaliq felt himself taken unawares by this impudent minx of a girl. How dared she answer him back—in a way which managed to be both insubordinate and yet smoothly diplomatic? Almost as if *she* had the upper hand! Why, he should show her who was boss…and…and…

Beneath his robes, he could feel himself growing hard and was just about to lock the door and take her into his arms until he realised such an action would throw his whole timetable out.

'Let's go!' he growled.

She followed him outside to where sat a low and gleaming car as scarlet and as bright as a sunset and Eleni looked at it suspiciously.

'Come on,' said Kaliq impatiently.

'What sort of machine is this?'

'It's a Maserati and it goes like a rocket.'

'But, Highness, I have no desire to travel in a rocket—'

'Just get in, will you?' he snapped.

What could she do but obey him?

'Hey,' said Kaliq softly as he roared off down the drive in a spray of gravel, relenting slightly as he saw her knuckles whiten in her lap. 'Just relax, little lizard.'

'How can I relax when you drive so fast?' she demanded hoarsely.

'Is that a criticism?'

'It's an observation.'

'You can go pretty fast yourself on a horse—I've seen you.'

'A horse is different—at least then I have some element of control.'

'You don't trust my driving, Eleni—is that it?'

'I'm not sure.'

'Oh?' He shot the one-word question at her.

Fear and all the conflicting emotions of the preceding night had loosened her tongue. Eleni shrugged. 'You have a reputation for being…'

'For being what?' he demanded.

'Nothing.'

'*Tell* me!'

Eleni wriggled in her seat. All the rules had been turned upside down—maybe if she offended him badly enough with the truth then he would have her shipped straight back to Calista and she would be liberated from the dangerous excitement of his company. 'Reckless,' she said reluctantly.

His mouth hardened. He knew that—for it was no secret. And on one level Kaliq had always revelled in his daredevil, playboy image. As a teenager, he had embraced risk and clung to it like an old friend. Adrenalin was his lifeblood—as was pushing life to its very limits. It had been his way of coping with a world made dark by the disappearance of his brother—and his guilt at the part he had played in it.

Yet he had to admit that as time had gone on he had found that risk could be wearing—even boring. But making that discovery for himself was one thing—having this little nobody pointing it out to him was quite another! He felt the fire of anger and indignation and something else he didn't quite recognise.

On impulse, he turned the car sharp left well

before they reached the main gates and then bumped down the lane into a shaded little copse before coming to a halt. He switched off the ignition and turned to look at her.

'This isn't the way to the polo field,' said Eleni slowly.

'No.'

'I thought you were worried we were going to be late for the polo.'

'I was.'

'Then…then what are we doing?'

'This,' he said fiercely. 'As you think I'm so reckless, then let me live up to my reputation.' And he leaned over her and began to kiss her with a passion so intense that she couldn't have stopped him, even if she'd wanted to.

Eleni went up in flames. It was as if he'd set her on fire with that first touch of his lips and hard embrace—so that when he caught her breast almost roughly in his hand she urged him on with a fervent, *'yes!'* And when he started pushing up her tunic and began to untie the belt of her trousers she found herself moaning her impatience—lifting her bottom to help him pull them down as if she had been born to be seduced in the cramped and confined space of a sports car.

And her eagerness seemed to ignite *him*— as if he needed any more encouragement! He groaned as he freed himself, so hard and so hot for her that he felt he might burst. If she had been more experienced, he might have just told her to take him in her mouth—but for some reason he found himself glad that she wasn't. He wanted *her*—to plunge deep into her tightness and lose himself.

Letting the seat down so that it was almost horizontal, he loosened his clothing and positioned himself so that he could enter her. And after that first delicious thrust, he stayed completely still for a moment—just revelling in the magnificent sense of filling her with himself, staring down at the darkening of her eyes and the slow pinkening of her cheeks.

'By the desert storm,' he murmured, and began to move inside her.

It all happened very quickly. It seemed only seconds before Eleni was gasping with the same sweet pleasure that she had so recently discovered—and something in her swift orgasm seemed to please him because she was half aware that he was watching her before finally he jerked against her body with a low, wild groan of his own.

He did not move. They stayed like that for seconds—or maybe it was minutes—until he had stilled inside her. He cradled her head against his chest with his hand, stroking it almost absently as he struggled to free himself from the dreamy lethargy which had settled over him like a soft blanket and was quite unlike anything he'd ever known before. How could it be that a functional and urgent coupling in his car could feel this good?

He wrapped a silken curl around his

finger. 'You learn very quickly,' he commented unsteadily.

Aware of a sudden danger—of the strange desire to tell him that he made her heart sing—Eleni pulled her head away from his chest. 'Am I to be judged like a horse in the field?' she questioned lightly.

His hand skated down to rest proprietorially on her bottom, letting it splay over the silken-soft skin. 'Well, you *do* have a magnificent flank,' he teased.

Automatically, she whispered her fingertips over the iron-hard muscle of his thigh. 'And so do you.'

Kaliq swallowed, feeling himself stir once again. It was bizarre how easily and how comfortably she had slipped into the shadowy world of intimacy, he thought—but her words reminded him of where he was, and who with. He glanced at the heavy gold timepiece which gleamed at his wrist. 'We had better get moving,' he said, his gaze raking over her critically. He sighed. She looked exactly like a woman who had just been ravaged in the back of a car. 'Can you repair your appearance?' he demanded.

The pleasure of that urgent coupling was shattered as surely as an egg dropping onto stones from a great height—spattering her with shame and the realisation of how she must look. How quickly he could change from ardent lover to cruel critic, she thought.

'I will do my best,' she said tightly.

As he reversed the car back along the road and renewed their journey Eleni sat and brushed her hair—not caring that he kept glancing at the abundant fall, like a snake fascinated by a charmer.

'You should wear it like that all the time,' he commented.

'It is not practical on horseback,' said Eleni tartly, for his earlier words had stung her.

'Are you angry with me?' Now why the hell was he asking her *that*?

'I just think it is unrealistic for you to expect me to look…neat…when you have been climbing all over me.'

Kaliq bit back a smile. He should be remonstrating with her for *daring* to berate her sheikh, not admiring her feistiness. 'I thought you liked me climbing all over you.'

'That isn't the point.'

They arrived just as the match was starting and at least the thundering of the horses' hooves on the grass was a welcome distraction from Eleni's distracted and erotic thoughts as she tried to ignore the towering presence of the dark sheikh at her side. Or the attention he was getting. The polo field was absolutely packed with spectators—including some of the most beautiful and outrageously dressed women she had ever seen.

And every single one of them seemed to be staring at Kaliq.

'All the women are looking at you,' she blurted out, before she could stop herself.

He gave the flicker of an arrogant smile. 'But of course they are,' he said, with a careless shrug. 'I excite the attention of women wherever I go—they are naturally drawn to my power and virility.' His black eyes glittered. 'You aren't displaying signs of jealousy, are you, Eleni?'

She heard the unmistakable warning in his voice and heeded it, even though the predatory look on the faces of the women was like rubbing salt on her already-raw senses. 'It is not my place to show signs of jealousy or possession, Highness,' she said meekly.

Kaliq's eyes narrowed. That submissive little tone of hers sounded suspiciously like insubordination, especially following on from her spirited responses in the car. 'Just make sure you don't,' he snapped.

Occasionally, the women looked at her, as well—and Eleni knew she wasn't imagining their undisguised disdain at her appearance. And suddenly she understood why Kaliq had warned her that she risked being patronised if she did not attempt to blend in. Had she really thought that this was going to be simple?

Until she forced herself to remember that none of these things mattered. *Your feelings do not count. You are here for one purpose and that is to offer him your expertise on the proposed purchase of a horse. The fact that you have allowed the sheikh to bed you and make frantic love to you in his car is of no consequence to him, or to you.*

'So which horse is it that you're thinking of buying?' she asked him, her calm voice in complete contrast to the tumult of her thoughts.

He glanced down at her, sensing that she was completely oblivious to the impact she'd just had—and was continuing to have—on his senses. The faint pink of post-coital flush highlighted her high cheekbones and her hair looked like a dark satin waterfall.

She looked, he realized, a million times more alluring than the women who watched him, with their breasts and legs on display as if parading themselves to the highest bidder. And the other men in the crowd were not oblivious to her appeal, either. She stood out like a bright and exotic flower in a subdued suburban garden.

He swallowed. Why, who would think with that cool sense of self-possession that she had been writhing beneath him in the Maserati only minutes earlier? He felt the hot leap of renewed desire and forced himself to concentrate on the horse. 'Which one do you think I favour?'

Eleni narrowed her eyes and searched the field. 'The bay, I'd say—the one in the yellow colours. He's certainly the most eye-catching.'

Kaliq smiled. 'Bravo,' he said softly. 'He's from Argentina—the home of the finest of all polo ponies. See how he moves.'

She fixed her eyes on the horse and watched him—a streak of pure muscle and agility as his rider urged him towards the goal.

'So what do you think?' asked Kaliq.

'He is indeed magnificent,' she replied, after a moment. 'He seems to follow the ball with his eyes, wherever it is on the field.'

'To watch the ball is the mark of a great polo pony!' said Kaliq triumphantly. 'You see, Eleni—you know nothing of polo and yet your instinct guides you towards the most important factor when determining whether to buy!'

At that moment the bay's rider scored a goal and the crowd erupted into polite applause.

'So shall I buy him, lizard?'

She looked at him. 'The sheikh is much too extravagant with his money! It is too early to say—I would need to ride him first.'

'That can be arranged.'

Eleni didn't speak any English, but it was very clear from the sceptical glances directed at her by the horse's owner after the match that he doubted her ability to ride such a towering creature.

Kaliq turned to her. 'He wants us to come back tomorrow—when the horse is fresh.'

'The best test of all is when a horse is tired,' said Eleni stubbornly. 'Tell him that five minutes is all I need—and I will be gentle with him.'

Kaliq's lips curved. 'Whatever the lady wants, the lady shall have.'

It shocked Eleni how thrilling she should find his compliment but why *shouldn't* he be flattering about her? Just because she wasn't high-born didn't mean that she shouldn't have the praise she assumed all men gave to lovers who pleased them.

And how to please him more? she wondered as she swung herself lightly up onto the bay. How to make herself the most unforgettable of all his bed-partners? So that he would always ache whenever he stopped to remember her.

It took just ten minutes for her to find out everything she needed to know about the horse and she jumped off, her face completely blank as she met the searching question searing at her from Kaliq's black eyes.

'You don't rate him?' he questioned shortly.

'I rate him very highly indeed. That bay is the finest horse I've ever ridden. He's light in the mouth and finely balanced—why, he responds so well that you could turn him on a market-trader's coin!'

'Then why the glum face?'

Eleni patted the animal's neck. 'I am aware that his owner is standing close by and while he cannot understand when we speak in our native tongue—he can certainly read the expression on our faces. And it is better that he thinks the worst. That way you will get a much better price for him, Highness.'

'I commend you,' Kaliq said, with a low laugh. 'But do you really think that a man in my position needs to *barter*, lizard?'

Eleni shrugged. 'I would have thought that pride would make you pursue the best possible price.'

His gaze ran over her with insolent appreciation. 'What a perfect find you have turned out to be,' he murmured. 'But don't you realise that your resourcefulness excites my sexual hunger? Suddenly I long to feel you in my arms and between my legs again.'

Eleni blushed. 'Highness, please stop it. For we are not alone—and there is your reputation to think of.'

'You must know that I've never cared about my reputation.'

'Maybe not, but I do care about mine. And there will be time enough for that later—when we are alone once more.'

'That's a promise, is it?' he questioned silkily.

Suddenly, Eleni found herself enjoying this game they seemed to be playing and she found that she was growing aroused herself. The steady beat of her heart accelerated and she wished that she could shout at the bay's owner and tell him to leave them in peace, so that she could pull her dark lover down onto a bed of straw and lie with him in the most basic of ways.

I want to kiss you, Kaliq, she thought with a fierce pang of longing—*I want to kiss you all over. I want to start with your lips and end with your toes and tell you that you are capturing my heart as surely as if you had thrown a silken net around it.*

But wasn't that what he had explicitly warned her against? Mistaking the pleasure he brought to her body for love itself? Eleni shut her eyes, forcing herself to concentrate on the physical. *His body is all you are allowed*, she reminded herself—*and that is only for a limited period.*

I need to make the most of my time with the sheikh, she thought, but her face showed nothing of the sudden fierce ache in her heart as she smiled up at him.

'Buy the horse,' she urged.

He nodded. 'I will take your advice.' He turned to the horse's owner and began speaking in English and the man said something else which caused Kaliq to frown.

'He doesn't want to sell?' questioned Eleni in surprise. 'What did he say?'

Kaliq looked at her assessingly before switching to Calistan. 'He said that he has never seen a woman display such skill in the saddle. And that if ever you could be tempted away from working for me—that he would offer you a job here.'

'Well, that's a compliment, isn't it?' said Eleni, wondering what had made his face darken with anger. 'A compliment to you, as well as to me?'

'It is not his place to try to poach the staff of the sheikh!' he retorted hotly.

Eleni felt the sting of humiliation. How insulting his words were—as if she was nothing more than a tiny cog, a part of the sheikh's huge workforce. *But that's all you are*, taunted the voice of reason. *All you ever will be. His employee. His horse girl.* Or was she really labouring under the illusion that sharing his body gave her any real rights in his life?

'He probably wants you in his bed, too!' Kaliq added.

Eleni felt sick. Not just his horse girl, but his sexual toy, too. Until he grew bored with her. And then she felt the shiver of ice over her skin as a fragmented future swam before her eyes. What would happen to her when that day came—when the prince cast her aside— when another lover caught his eye and his imagination? Eleni swallowed down the acid taste of fear as she looked at him.

'The man is about sixty,' she said coldly.

Their eyes met. 'You think that a virile man's sexual desire is ever diminished by age?' he questioned, on an arrogant boast.

Eleni swallowed. 'I hadn't given it much thought,' she said listlessly.

His eyes narrowed. What was the matter with her now? Did she not realise that her place was to smile and to please him—not to stand before him creasing her creamy skin with a frown? Perhaps he would just have to show her and drive the lesson home. 'Come on. Let's go. I'm taking you home to bed,' he said roughly.

CHAPTER ELEVEN

'K…KALIQ! Oh, Kaliq! *Oh!*'

Waiting until the last of her breathless spasms had shuddered against his tongue, Kaliq moved up over Eleni's naked body and looked down at her flushed face.

'You liked that, I think?' he murmured.

Her flush deepened, her lashes fluttering down to conceal her embarrassment. 'Y-yes.'

'Look at me,' Kaliq commanded.

How could she possibly look at him after what he had just done to her? But knowing that he would insist until she capitulated, Eleni reluctantly stared into the mocking ebony of his gaze, scarcely able to believe that the sheikh had been kissing her *there* and what gasping pleasure it had brought her. Another shudder racked through her naked body and she swallowed. 'Oh, Kaliq—is such a thing not…not…'

'Not what, my beauty?'

'Oh, I don't know…I don't know.' She didn't seem to know anything any more. '*Wr-wrong*, I suppose.'

He stroked her breast and felt its bud tighten against his questing finger. 'Why should it be wrong?' he queried softly.

'Because it seems *wicked*, somehow.' She wriggled her shoulders. 'And because it feels so good.' Just as everything they seemed to have spent this past week doing had felt good. Too good, really. Once again she felt the cold wash of fear which had begun to increasingly haunt her. How on earth was she going to be able to cope once her time with Kaliq was over?

Reflectively, he stroked a long wave of dark silken hair from her damp cheek. 'But sex sometimes does feel wicked,' he agreed. 'That is part of its allure. The sense of the forbidden. The illicit.' And the unexpected, he thought suddenly. Because Eleni had confounded him. He had never expected it to be this amazing. By now he should be growing bored with her body. Her voice should be sounding shrill to his ears. He should be looking for excuses to increasingly avoid her except for night-time—when, perplexingly, the opposite was true.

He found himself seeking her out. Luring her back into bed when they had only just left it. And discovering that she was learning the skills of sex with astonishing speed.

Her words cut into his thoughts. 'And does it always feel this good?'

Now it was his turn to close his eyes, mainly to block out the irresistible question in hers. Her innocence was part of her own allure, as was her endless curiosity and willingness to learn. He could never recall being so relaxed and easy in a woman's arms.

When he asked her opinion—even though asking a humble stable girl was in itself madness—she expressed it honestly. With Eleni it was as if he had stumbled upon a dark stone in the desert sand and had cleaned it up to discover that a precious gem lay beneath.

There was true intimacy between them, he realised—with something approaching dismay. And wasn't there a part of him which wished she *had* experienced other lovers? So that this sense of sweet *wonder* she displayed in his arms did not exist—and he could have mocked and taunted her with questions about how the other men matched up to him. So that he would be spared any fleeting guilt when the time came to cast her aside.

'You ask too many questions!' he complained.

'But I thought you liked me to ask questions.'

'Not always. Now you must return the favour,' he instructed, without opening his eyes.

Sensing that she had somehow displeased him, Eleni wriggled down and began to butterfly her lips over his torso the way he had taught her to do. She felt him writhe as she touched her tongue to his salty hardness—and he groaned and tangled his hands in her hair.

But even as she put her new-found sexual skills into practice she felt a wrench of heartache which was never too far from the surface. For it was bittersweet to acknowledge the topsy-turvy element which her life had taken on since she had become the sheikh's lover. Physically, she was glowing like a lamp and feeling on a constant high— but emotionally, she was all over the place.

A week in England had been like a whole lifetime in miniature—a lifetime she never wanted to end. She shared the prince's bed and ate her meals exclusively with him—and in between times, he had shown her a little of England. On his luxury jet they had flown to York and to Cambridge—when Kaliq took her to look over some of the other horses he was thinking of adding to his stables.

'I want my polo club to be the most presti-gious in the world,' he told her. 'To bring the best kind of tourism to Calista—and to benefit its people.'

And then what? Eleni wondered—though she didn't dare ask. His nature was so restless she suspected that nothing—no achievement in the world—would ever satisfy him.

His life was full of acquisitions, she realised. The garage full of gleaming cars. The light aircraft he kept on a nearby airfield was rarely used and neither was the yacht which was moored down on the south coast, kept per-fectly ready and waiting for one of his infre-quent visits.

'When *do* you sail?' she asked him one day.

'When the sea is at its most challenging.'

His answer did not surprise her. Risk was his most constant partner, she realised for-lornly—as much a part of his character as his passion and lust for life. Was that why he refused the services of bodyguards wherever possible? Why he drove too fast and jumped his horses too high?

She kept wondering when he would take her back to Calista, but she was too scared to ask that, too—terrified that a wrong word would make it come to pass even sooner. Deep down she recognised that her time as his lover was surely coming to an end. For a man used to the most beautiful and wealthy women in the world—wouldn't he soon begin to grow bored with his country girl? Especially now that she no longer even had the lure of her virginity to commend her. Maybe the sooner that day came around, the better it would be for her.

Because now, as she lay in his bed, pleasuring him, with the light from the afternoon sun gilding their naked bodies, Eleni realised she had fallen into the very trap he had warned her about. Somewhere along the way she had fallen in love with him. Except that Kaliq had made it sound like a reaction—a woman justifying sex by convincing herself that she was in love.

But this didn't feel like justification. It didn't feel like a woman who was ashamed of her behaviour and so tagged on an acceptable label to it.

It felt real. As real as the rain on her face, or the wind streaming through her hair when she galloped along the hard desert sands.

The feelings she had for him felt as powerful and as constant as the sun. Feelings she had to spend most of her time fighting. She found herself wanting to shower his skin with tiny kisses and to stroke away the deep grooves which sometimes creased his brow when he was deep in thought. To pull his beloved dark head to her breast—to comfort and to love him, as well as to gently run her fingers through his ruffled black hair.

I love him, she thought helplessly. *I love him with a power which makes the rest of life seem inadequate.*

She tried to talk herself out of it, telling herself that she had simply become bewitched by the unbelievable position in which she found herself—of being the prince's lover. Beneath her supposedly practical, horsey exterior—perhaps she was really one of those women who were secretly swayed by wealth. Who liked all the fine things which money could buy. The hot water running from the shiny taps. The pure silk robes. The best horses to ride, and food served on golden plates.

Maybe she wasn't so down-to-earth as she'd always thought, but was secretly entertaining unrealistic dreams about her future. Was she contemplating what it might be like to be a permanent fixture in the life of her sheikh?

But even as she allowed the thoughts to filter into her mind, Eleni knew that they did not represent the person she really was, or what she really felt deep inside. If Kaliq turned around and told her that he was going to turn his back on all his royal riches and privilege—wouldn't she more than happily take his hand and walk off into the unknown future with him? In fact, didn't part of her long for just such an unlikely scenario? Knowing that would be the only way for her to have any kind of future with him.

But, in reality, there wasn't going to be a future.

Pleasure overtook him and Kaliq groaned as his seed spilled into her mouth, then he pulled her up to lie on top of him as she licked her lips like a kitten. 'Who taught you to do that?' he shuddered.

'You did.'

'What else did I teach you?'

'This.'

Boldly, she leaned over and planted her lips on his and he could taste his own muskiness on her mouth as she kissed him so sweetly that it felt uncomfortably close to poignant. He certainly didn't remember teaching her to do *that*. Kissing was something he always kept to a minimum. It brought up feelings he had pushed away or long forgotten. Kissing was almost *too* intimate—far more intimate than sex itself. Too close to emotion and he didn't do emotion. And yet…

He lay back against the rumpled bed-sheets—and, for once in his life, remained passive to the soft ministrations of her mouth. Just this once he would allow her a moment of tenderness and allow himself to become tangled in its dangerous web.

Just for a moment, he kissed her back—without restraint or reservation—a soft warmth beginning to heat the blood in his veins as he did so. With a moan of delight she wrapped her arms and her legs around him and deepened that silent kiss.

On and on that sweet kiss continued, until he moaned her name softly into her mouth, and as the sound of the phone jangled loudly on the bedside table Kaliq pulled away from her with something approaching relief.

'I thought you told Zahra you didn't want to be disturbed by anyone,' blurted out Eleni before she could stop herself, aware that the tantalising spell had been broken.

His black eyes glittered out a distinct warning—sending out the unspoken message that it was not *her* place to question him. 'It is obviously someone who's insisting on speaking to me. Which must mean one of my brothers.' Raking his fingers through his ruffled black hair, he lifted up the receiver and listened.

'Oh, it's you, Zakari,' he said drily. 'Are you disturbing me? Well, yes—as a matter of fact, you are.' He fixed his gaze on Eleni's bare and rosy breasts and his eyes narrowed. 'Would you like to call back later? No, I thought not.' He listened for a few moments, and then gave an odd kind of smile as he replaced the phone.

'Is everything…okay?' asked Eleni.

He yawned and stretched his arms above his head. 'That depends on how you feel about the imminent arrival of my elder brother.'

'Sheikh Zakari?' Eleni's eyes widened in horror as reality began to close in like a vice clamping around her throat. 'You mean he's coming *here*?'

'Apparently. He's been in London speaking to some diamond expert, heard that I was in the country and has decided to call in for dinner.'

Eleni sat bolt upright, her hair tumbling down over her breasts, her heart beating out a frantic rhythm. 'Then I will hide myself away until he is gone!'

Kaliq looked at her. At that moment she looked uniquely lovely—all flushed and rumpled from an afternoon in bed but with that natural grace and elegance which was all her own. Someday soon she would no longer be his lover, but in the meantime it seemed a little unnecessary that he shouldn't be able to feast his eyes on her while he still had the opportunity. And suddenly an audacious idea occurred to him.

'Why not stay and meet him for yourself?' he questioned slowly.

Eleni blinked at him in disbelief but his

words only reminded her of her situation. That she was nothing but a lowly servant and Calista's most powerful man was coming for dinner! *She* meet Zakari! Was Kaliq out of his mind to suggest such a thing?

'Meet the Sheikh Zakari? But I could not possibly do that!'

'Why not?'

'Because…because he is the king and he will not approve of a lowly stable girl having…having…' she searched around wildly for the right word—because surely *relationship* was far too presumptuous a term '…*sex* with his younger brother.'

It was a curiously insulting and bald little phrase for her to have used, Kaliq thought, with a flicker of irritation. 'I wasn't planning to announce it over dinner,' he said sarcastically.

'N-no. No, of course not,' she stumbled, aware that now she *had* been presumptuous.

'Of course, we could always play a little game,' he suggested carelessly.

'A game?' Eleni looked at him suspiciously. 'What…what kind of game?'

The black eyes glittered. 'Look at how relaxed you have become in my company,' he murmured. 'So why not see how far your un-doubted talents can stretch. Do you think you can play hostess for me while I entertain my brother for dinner?'

She stared at him. 'But surely he would not approve of a…*stable girl* playing hostess to the ruling family!' protested Eleni.

'Then don't tell him. Imply that you're a Calistan noblewoman—perhaps the daughter of one of our diplomatic staff. Be vague. I can assure you that he will not be interested enough to pursue the matter.'

'But is that not…dishonest?' questioned Eleni uncertainly.

Kaliq's lips curved. 'Less dishonest surely than hiding you away with the rest of the staff as if you are nothing at all to me.'

She could read the challenge in his black

eyes. *But I* am *nothing to you*, she reminded herself—and the painful understanding helped make her mind up. In bed at least, she was his equal—so why not grab at this chance to pretend she was equal in all ways? An evening of make-believe. For once she could pretend to be a real princess. A glimpse of the life she would never get a chance to lead.

Wasn't this an opportunity to banish her feelings of inferiority once and for all—to prove that she *was* as good as her Kaliq? And wasn't there a wistful corner of her heart which longed for him to acknowledge that fact, too?

Eleni swallowed down her fears and nodded. In theory it would be no different from mounting a temperamental horse—you just had to adapt to the challenge it presented. She would show her royal lover that she was fit to grace his dinner table as hostess—but most of all she would prove it to herself. 'Very well, Kaliq,' she agreed steadily. 'I will meet your brother.'

CHAPTER TWELVE

'AND this is Eleni,' Kaliq glimmered her a narrow-eyed look. 'Eleni, I'd like you to meet the Sheikh Zakari Al'Farisi.'

Trying to quell her nerves, Eleni bobbed a deep curtsey at the tall man who had just swept into the room at Kaliq's side, then slowly lifted her eyes to his face. For only servants were obliged to remain staring at the ground she reminded herself.

At first, it was easy to tell that the two men were brothers—they had the same glittering black eyes, the same beak-like noses and those high, autocratic cheekbones. But Zakari's mouth was slightly fuller—and it was completely unsmiling.

His intelligent gaze raked over her and for a moment Eleni was acutely aware of what she was doing—pretending to be something she wasn't, and thereby entering into a deception against the oldest of the Al'Farisi brothers. Was that an offence against the royal family? she wondered. And was Kaliq just using her to play her off against his brother for some reason unknown to her?

She knew that the hard-faced sheikh was betrothed to the beautiful but headstrong Princess Kalila. So he was used to mixing with women of pure royal blood, she reminded herself—and surely that meant he would see right through her? And realise that beneath all the expensive finery she wore— she was nothing but a humble stable girl?

For a moment her nerve almost failed her and she thought seriously about fleeing from the room—until she reminded herself that she *was* Kaliq's lover. And surely that gave her some sort of right to be there? Why, if Calistan society was not so stupidly rigid—then she could have played hostess just by being herself. *So why not try to enjoy this one opportunity you have to play Kaliq's princess for the evening?*

'I am truly honoured to make the acquaintance of the King of Calista,' she said softly.

Zakari frowned. 'But I thought we were dining on our own.'

Kaliq slammed his brother an imperturbable look. 'And I thought a little feminine company might enliven the evening—and, besides, Eleni is very discreet.'

'Is she?' Zakari looked at her again, more speculatively this time. 'She is certainly very beautiful.'

This time Eleni *did* lower her eyelids modestly—it hid her surprise at Zakari's comment and at least it blocked out the black glare being directed at her by her lover.

But as they sat down at the table she was aware of how different this very special finery made her feel. Why, she almost *felt* like a real princess tonight—for she had dressed for the part, determined to play her role with aplomb. She had worn the most delicate robes in her wardrobe—finest silk in softest rose-pink, overlaid with intricate and exquisite gold embroidery. And Kaliq had insisted on sending out for jewellery to match.

It had astonished Eleni that a few terse instructions barked down a telephone could translate into an armoured car appearing just over an hour later—with a heavily guarded man bearing velvet-lined trays of glittering gems.

'Take your pick,' Kaliq commanded.

Eleni's instinct was to choose the most modest of the offerings on show—although even those must have cost a king's ransom—but Kaliq had other ideas.

'No. Wear these.' And he plucked out a necklace of bright rubies and diamonds and slipped it around her neck. 'All ice and fire—just like you, my sweet beauty.'

His words made her melt with longing and Eleni's fingers were trembling as she clipped on the matching earrings and studded her piled-up hair with jewelled hairpins. Zahra insisted on lending her a kohl pencil and showed her how to draw a subtle dark line around her eyes. How scarily huge it made them look! When she was finally ready, Eleni looked into the mirror and barely recognised the dazzling creature who stared back at her.

'Do I…do I look okay?' she asked Kaliq.

'Oh, yes…you look okay,' he echoed, and Kaliq's mouth twisted into a grim kind of smile. He had wondered what she might look like in make-up and finery and now he knew, and perversely he wanted to tell her to scrub the whole lot off again. 'So okay,' he said unevenly, 'that I would like to remove all those fine jewels and fine clothes and take my Eleni back to bed—for while you look very good when you're all dressed up, you look best in nothing at all.'

His words, as usual, disarmed and alarmed her. Words meant nothing. And Kaliq saying something like *my* Eleni was simply a term of possession, nothing more.

During the meal, Eleni ate sparingly of the lavish feast provided—her stomach was too fluttery with nerves for her to have any real appetite—but to her surprise she found she was able to hold her own while talking to King Zakari. They spoke of horses, and the great literature of Calistan. And she found herself discussing new falcon-rearing methods and the impact they would have on one of Calista's favourite sports.

'So just who *are* you, Eleni?' Zakari asked eventually—pushing away his half-eaten dish of pomegranate sorbet.

Kaliq glowered—for hadn't his brother already spent much of the meal monopolising Eleni? And hadn't she been allowing him to do so with an enthusiasm which was completely inappropriate? 'I wasn't aware that you had come to talk about my guest,' Kaliq snapped.

'And I wasn't aware that you were so unusually sensitive about your guest's welfare,' returned Zakari.

'So are you here to pass the time of day, or is there a reason behind your visit?' demanded Kaliq hotly.

The brothers' eyes met in a moment of silent, sibling battle before Zakari shrugged. 'It is true. I have come to England in search of jewels which are alleged to have been stolen from our royal palaces many years ago. But in truth, I am weary of jewels and their significance to our islands.' His voice dropped and he shot Eleni another quick glance before continuing. 'When I was at the king's funeral—I discovered that one half of the Stefani diamond is missing.'

Kaliq gave a low laugh. 'So what? There are enough diamonds in both kingdoms not to miss one, surely—no matter how magnificent.'

'I don't think you understand the significance, Kaliq,' said Zakari slowly. 'The Coronation of the new King of Aristo cannot take place until the missing half of the Stefani diamond has been found.'

Kaliq's eyes narrowed. 'And the implication to that is...*what*?' he questioned softly.

'I shall not rest until I find it,' declared Zakari fervently. 'It shall fall to *my* hand to discover it—not Sebastian! And then my greatest wish shall be achieved—for with the discovery of that precious jewel I shall reunite the two halves of the Stefani diamond and I shall reunite the islands in the name of our beloved stepmother, Queen Anya.'

Eleni blinked. This was highly confidential information from the lips of the king himself! And it was at that moment she knew she could no longer intrude on their conversation—not now that it seemed to have taken a dramatic and highly personal twist, judging by their sombre expressions.

She had no place here at this table any more. She and Kaliq had succeeded in their little game and Zakari had been comfortable enough to spend the evening dining with her—oblivious to her real and lowly position in life. Suddenly, she felt more than a little disturbed. What on earth had been the point of taking part in such an unnecessary deception? She rose from the table, ignoring Kaliq's sudden look of query.

'Please excuse me,' she said quietly. 'You both have important matters of State to discuss and it is not for me to intrude on them. I bid you good evening, Sheikh Zakari, and am honoured to have made your acquaintance,' she said, and bent low in another formal curtsey.

'The honour was indeed mine,' murmured Zakari as he rose to his feet and bowed.

Clutching a fold of her gown between thumb and forefinger, Eleni left the room with her head held high, but as she closed the great wooden doors behind her she heard the unmistakable words which Zakari uttered.

'She's your lover, isn't she?'

There was a pause. 'You think I would have someone that beautiful staying in my house and not bed her?' Kaliq was saying.

Zakari's tone was thoughtful. 'But there is something you're not telling me.'

Eleni knew that to listen was wrong—but was there another woman in the world who would not have done the same under the circumstances?

Kaliq laughed. 'You won't believe me if I do!' And then he lowered his voice and began to speak.

She heard the words *stable girl* and something else and Zakari's small exclamation of disbelief. Eleni leaned against the door and salt tears welled up and blurred her vision as she tried to blot out Kaliq's hateful and boastful tone. Her eyes closed. How he must be laughing at her now. How could he? How *could* he?

Was he bragging about how he had broken in his little stable girl—taken her virginity and then schooled her in the art of love-making, just as you would school a newly broken horse? Showing off to his older brother as if she was some kind of amusing diversion! But what had she expected? What an utter fool she had been to imagine that there had been some kind of special bond between her and Kaliq. She had only believed that because it was what she *wanted* to believe, and not because it was true.

And what would the powerful Zakari think of his brother's behaviour? Because Kaliq had not only bedded someone completely unsuited to a royal sheikh, but had allowed her to entertain his powerful brother—and surely that was an almighty risk for him to have taken?

And then it hit her so hard that she wondered how she could have been so stupid not to have thought of it before.

Of course it was a risk, she realised. For

wasn't that the motivation behind *all* Kaliq's behaviour? Because risk made the mundane tolerable, didn't it—as well as providing excitement for the jaded appetite of a rich and powerful man?

Hurt and pain and betrayal clutched at her heart like a cold vise and in her bedroom she wanted to tear the dazzling jewellery from her neck but dared not mishandle it for fear it would break. And so it was with trembling fingers that she carefully removed the necklace, earrings and clips and replaced them in the velvet-lined box. Never had the temporary nature of her situation been driven home so starkly as when she took off those borrowed gemstones. Then she hung up her clothes and slipped into a silken robe— because she was damned if she would wait naked in the bed for her sheikh like some sacrificial lamb.

Her heart was pounding as she heard the distant slamming of the heavy front door, the sound of footsteps approaching her bedroom. Drawing in a deep breath, she waited to see if he would knock—but of course he didn't. Why should he show her any courtesy, when deep down she was nothing more than a servant in his eyes, no matter how priceless the jewels he gave her to wear nor how easily she could fool his brother into thinking otherwise?

Kaliq entered the room, his lips curving into a speculative smile as he saw her standing—robed—by the writing desk. Her long hair tumbled down to her waist in a dark, silken cloud and the rich satin clung like melted butter to her slender curves. His voice dipped into a caress even as he felt the sing of blood in his veins as he observed her. 'You aren't tired?'

'Should I be?'

His eyes narrowed as something unfamiliar in her tone alerted him to the fact that all was not well. 'The dinner must have been something of an endurance for you.'

She turned round then, her green eyes full

of hurt. 'You think so?' she whispered. 'Perhaps it was a triumph that I managed to endure it without disgracing myself? Without picking up a chicken bone and gnawing at it like an animal! No doubt you are amazed you could trust your stable girl to behave herself in the most daunting of circumstances—or that your brother should deign to sit down and share a meal with me in the first place.'

A nerve began to flicker at Kaliq's temple as he felt the first steal of anger. 'Don't be ridiculous, Eleni,' he said steadily. 'My brother liked you very much.'

'Until you told him who I was?' she said flatly.

'What the hell are you talking about?' he questioned icily.

'You've…you've told him who I really am, haven't you, Kaliq?'

There was a pause. 'And if I have?'

For some reason Eleni wanted to scream—and yet reason was playing no part in this great swirling mass of emotions which now made her heart feel as if someone were tearing at it with their jagged fingernails.

'And wh-what *exactly* did you tell him?' she questioned shakily. 'That I was your adaptable little stable girl who you schooled and then dressed up like a glittering puppet so that she could fool the world and the royal family into thinking she was more than she really is?'

'What I told him is my business!' he flared back. 'And certainly not yours to question. How dare you speak to me in this manner?'

But Eleni ignored the dark note in his voice—some force far stronger than common sense driving her on to say her piece. 'Because I'm angry,' she answered. 'And because I'm hurt. We're lovers, Kaliq—and that should make us equal, but of course it doesn't! And I'm not talking about the differences in our circumstances, but real equality. Because if we were *truly* equal, then I should have the freedom to tell you what's on my mind—even if you don't agree with it.'

'And just what exactly *is* on your mind?' he questioned dangerously.

Eleni heard the abrasive edge to his voice and some tiny corner of her heart urged her to stop now, before it was too late. Before she said something irrevocable which he would never be able to forgive. Before things changed for ever.

But hadn't they changed anyway, all on their own? The way things always *did* change, because nothing in life ever stayed the same. The flowers in the desert which bloomed and died were just different versions of their own small lives. Her brief and beautiful affair with the prince was almost over; she had known that the sands of time were running out on it almost from the moment it had first begun and she must accept that.

And Eleni knew that she was in much too far not to tell him—and wouldn't it be dishonest to *herself* if she didn't go through with it? To do what—to curtsey to her sheikh as if nothing had happened—to put it all from her mind and carry on as before? Letting him strip her bare and make love to her as if she had no feelings to hurt? How could she?

'Did you enjoy letting me play-act at being your hostess tonight?' she queried shakily. 'Or did you simply enjoy the risk that it involved—because risk is your whole reason for living, isn't it, Kaliq? It's the reason you went ahead and told Zakari I was your lover—even though there was no real need to. He'll never meet me again after tonight—we both know that. But maybe you were hoping for some kind of reaction? Your brother's envy that you should have been openly flaunting your affair with a servant—or his disapproval, perhaps?'

'That is *enough*!' he gritted furiously.

But Eleni couldn't stop the words which were tumbling out—because hadn't this aspect of his character troubled her for as long as they had been intimate? 'It's almost as if you want to bring discord into your life where none exists,' she whispered. 'As if that will make up for the fact that you've never forgiven yourself for Zafir's disappearance—'

'I said, that is *enough*!' he raged, catching her arms between the tight grip of his hands and pushing his face close to hers, his black eyes spitting angry fire. 'Understand?'

But Eleni wasn't afraid. She had lived with a man far more intimidating than this one and, stupidly, she just happened to love this one. She loved him so much that, even though she knew there was no future for them, she owed it to Kaliq to tell him a few home truths which nobody else had ever had the courage to tell him, and perhaps never would.

'No, it is *not* enough,' she returned, and as she saw the sheer amazement on his face that she had dared to contradict him her heart began to soften. For Kaliq was a product of his own upbringing and how could she blame him for being autocratic and demanding when that was exactly how he'd been taught to behave?

In an instant, all her anger and her bitterness fled and her voice lowered with gentle compassion as she sought to make him understand.

'When are you going to accept that Zafir's disappearance was *not your fault*, my darling?' she questioned quietly. 'Sometimes things happen in life and there is nothing you can do to prevent them. And unless you can accept that—then you are just going to carry on pushing life to the very limits until you take one risk too far, and perhaps end it prematurely.' She had to focus very hard to stop her voice from catching. 'Is that what you want, Kaliq?'

For a minute he stared at her, almost marvelling at her courage and clarity of thought until he reminded himself of the unforgivable *insolence* of her words and all the still-raw wounds they had opened.

He drew himself up and asserted every imperious inch of regal authority—wanting to lash out at her. To make her hurt just as she had hurt him. 'I think you forget yourself!' he bit out furiously. 'I do not discuss such matters with one of my *servants*. It is not your place to dictate to your sheikh, nor to *dare* suggest how I should or should not behave. Do you think that a girl from a desert shack knows better than her royal master?'

Eleni gasped as the cruel barbs of his words stung against her skin like tiny arrows. His face was dark with rage, his merciless dismissal of her flooding over her like a black tide.

'It is not your opinion nor affection that I want,' he continued. 'Never forget that! In fact, there is only one thing I want from you, Eleni Lakis, and we both know what that is!'

And with a low kind of roar, he bent and picked her up—so unexpectedly that it took her completely off guard, for what woman would have anticipated him wanting sex after such a tirade against her? He carried her effortlessly towards her bedroom—kicking the door open with his foot.

CHAPTER THIRTEEN

IN KALIQ'S arms Eleni trembled as he carried her towards the bed, biting her lip to quell her tears because fierce pride determined that he would not see her cry. *He would not*! All that courage she had mustered up to tell him the truth and yet all he was doing was ignoring it as he placed her down and…and…

'Kaliq—'

'Not now!' he bit out, but he could not seem to rid himself of the memory of her words, which still echoed round and round in his head as he stared down at her—at her green eyes so wide and bright.

Trying not to react to the candid scrutiny of his gaze, Eleni shuddered with a terrible kind of longing as he stood towering over her. Wanting him and trying *not* to want him. And then he bent to tip her chin up with the tips of his fingers as he stared down into her face, his eyes splinteringly cold—his mouth as hard as stone.

'Kaliq,' she breathed again. The word sounded miraculously calm—it was both statement and entreaty—for surely he would sense the utter uselessness in prolonging this agony?

His heart thundered with rage but his anger was tempered by the silky warmth of her sweet flesh and he slid down onto the bed beside her, pulling her up against his aroused body. 'I will forgive you your impertinence just this once, lizard—but you will never speak to your sheikh in such a way again, do you understand?' he whispered against her. 'Now come here and kiss me instead!'

Eleni could have wept. So much for delivering a few home truths. Everything she had said to him he'd just brushed away dismissively as if it didn't matter.

Because it *didn't* matter—not to him. And *she* didn't matter, either. Her thoughts or opinions were of no consequence—hadn't he just told her that himself? No matter that she wore the sheikh's fine clothes or was lent his priceless jewellery—she would never be anything more than the humble stable girl he had plucked from obscurity. A willing bed-partner to be taken when and wherever it pleased him.

But she still had her pride. Eleni swallowed. Was she prepared to let the man she loved go on taking and taking from her, until she had nothing left to give and was an empty shell of a woman—heartbroken and ready to be discarded?

Like hell she was! On horseback she was as fearless as any man—and she would dig deep for some of that fearlessness now. She met his eyes with a steady gaze, concentrating on keeping her body stiff and unresponsive, even though his hands were now cupping her breasts and making them ache with familiar desire. 'Kaliq—'

'Not now!' he husked as, with a small, angry moan, he drove his mouth down onto the erect bud of her nipple, sucking at it and teasing it through the slippery silk of the robe she wore. And as his mouth worked such sweet magic he was tangling his hands in her hair—coiling the thick strands around his scarred wrists as if they were silken ropes. 'Not now, my sweet Eleni!' he groaned against her.

Hot desire flowed from him into her and inside Eleni's heart began to melt like a candle left out in the midday sun. But somehow she fought against it. Resisting the power of his lips, she stayed still and unmoving in his arms—fighting desire and this hopeless swell of love for him. Because this was far more important than mere desire.

Deep down, she knew that their affair was over—so how on earth could she have empty, angry sex with him now? Wouldn't that just cheapen everything they had shared? If all she was to have of her sheikh were memories— then let them at least be golden ones and not the bitter remains of their angry row.

Kaliq sensed her resistance and let her go, raising his head from her breast—his black eyes narrowed and watchful as his heart pounded in his chest. 'Are you trying to make a point, Eleni?'

'But there is no point, is there, Kaliq?' she said quietly. 'Not any more. After all the angry words we've just exchanged—is it not best just to let it end here and now?'

His groin wanted to explode. What the hell was she talking about? She wanted him—she always wanted him, just as he always wanted her. More than any other woman he'd ever had, he realised—his pounding heart giving a sudden lurch.

'You think so?' he murmured, his lips moving to graze the silken field of skin above her breast, waiting for her arms to wind sinuously around his neck—but they did no such thing even though he felt her tremble beneath his caress.

He began to skate the flat of his hand down over the sleek curves of her hips and then possessively let it rest in between the softness of her thighs, anticipating the broken little moan she always made whenever he touched her there.

But no sound came even though he could hear the instinctive quickening of her breath. He moved to an even more intimate destination and yet, even though there she was soft and honeyed with welcome, she remained as still as if she had been fashioned from a block of ice. His passionate bed-partner had been replaced by a snow queen! Kaliq's eyes narrowed as he saw the wanton thrust of her breasts against the soft silk of her gown—recognising that her mind and her body were in conflict.

'Eleni?' he said softly.

Eleni met his gaze without flinching even

though her heart was racing with love and fear. 'Yes, Kaliq?'

'You are refusing me?' he questioned incredulously.

'I'm tr-trying to,' she answered honestly, praying that she could keep her tears at bay for just a little longer. 'Though if you insist on seducing me, we both know that I will be unable to resist you.'

The honesty of her words took Kaliq by surprise—though why should he have been surprised by that? Hadn't Eleni always been honest with him? More honest than any of his court would ever have dared be—but then sometimes he thought she was more courageous and more daring than the lot of them put together.

And yet she was strong enough to admit that she would be unable to resist him—and, oh, how he was tempted to prove her right. To begin a slow and merciless seduction and have her crying out her orgasm. To feel her tremble with surrender beneath him. But suddenly

Kaliq realised that such a victory would be an empty one, which would leave no lasting satisfaction. That he did not want only *part* of Eleni—the physical part—he wanted *her*. All of her. The all which she gave to him so generously every time they came together.

An unknown and unexpected pain ripped through him and he clenched his fists as if trying to fight the uncomfortable emotions which were pricking at his skin. Emotions which had begun to wither when his brother's birth had resulted in the death of their mother and which had died completely when that same brother had disappeared off the face of the earth.

Since then Kaliq had blocked out people as ruthlessly as he had blocked out emotion and now he understood why. Because this was what happened when you allowed someone to get too close—you started to *feel* things. You opened yourself up to hurt. And life was easier without that hurt.

He pulled away from her, his voice

sounding harsh. 'So now you play the games of the mistress, do you, Eleni? Using sex as a weapon?'

Registering his cruel taunt with disbelief, Eleni watched as he got up from the bed, his critical assessment ringing in her ears. And yet she had pushed him to this, hadn't she? She had no one to blame but herself for the fact that he was now walking towards the door. And just as he opened it he turned back—his black eyes as flinty and as unreadable as on that first day when he had galloped out of the desert sunset and into her life.

'How well you have learnt your lesson, my beauty,' he said softly. And then he was gone.

Eleni stared at the connecting bedroom door as it closed implacably behind him. He didn't slam it; perhaps it might have made her feel better if he had—a final show of passion rather than a quiet, dispiriting click.

And then reaction set in. Even though she could hear him moving around in the next room, Kaliq was gone. Gone from her life for ever—and a tearing pain made her want to howl aloud, like an animal left wounded in the desert. But she did not dare make a sound—for fear that he might hear her. Because her heart might be broken and her future uncertain—but she would conduct herself with dignity.

For a while she just lay on the bed where he had left her, trying to still her quickened breathing, trying to tell herself that everything was going to be all right—even if she didn't really believe it. She could hear the tick of the clock, feel the stickiness of the humid air, and Eleni realised that she was as trapped as she had ever been in her father's house. Alone in a strange room within a strange world—with a long and probably sleepless night ahead of her. And who knew what the morning and the future would bring?

And glancing down at her watch, she saw that only twenty minutes had passed! She felt the tears begin to well up behind her eyelids and she longed to cry, to drum at the walls with the fists of her hands. To let out some of this terrible, tearing pain which was clutching at her heart.

Her breath was tight in her dry throat, the sensation of choking as believable as the one which made her feel as if the walls were closing in on her—and Eleni knew that she had to get out of there, out into the space and fresh air of the gardens. At least there she could give into the tears which were welling up in her eyes without Kaliq having the satisfaction of knowing that he had made her cry. And his security guards would be patrolling the grounds—she would be safe enough.

Pulling on a tunic and trousers, she wrapped a soft cashmere shawl tightly around her shoulders because she was shivering—though more from emotional exhaustion than from cold. And then she slid her feet into a pair of embroidered slippers and crept from the room, closing the door softly behind her.

Listening for a moment but hearing only silence, Eleni slipped down the large and shadowed staircase, leaving by the front door and out into the night.

The sky was thick with clouds which were obscuring the dull light of the moon and the atmosphere felt still and heavy. Glancing upwards, she could see that Kaliq's light was still on and she saw his shadowy silhouette appear. A fierce pain ripped through her heart and she began to stumble away from the lights as the first drops of rain fell onto her bare head.

And somewhere in the distance, she heard the sound of dogs beginning to bark.

CHAPTER FOURTEEN

KALIQ stilled as the raucous barking of the dogs set his senses jangling—though they had been alerted to danger minutes before. Even in the midst of his troubled thoughts he had thought he'd heard a sound which was something out of the ordinary.

Striding across the vast master bedroom, he pushed open the interconnecting door to Eleni's bedroom, but as soon as his eyes scoured the room the rumpled sheets and the silence told him what he already knew. She was gone.

The barking of the dogs increased and he began to hurry from the room, down the stairs, hitting the alert button which he always carried and dragging the mobile phone from his pocket as he attempted to make contact with the bodyguards. But there was no reply and he suspected that they heard neither. That they were all caught up with investigating what had alerted the dogs—not knowing that it was Eleni. He'd even purposefully dismissed his personal bodyguards because he had been expecting to spend the night in the blissful anonymity of his lover's arms.

He ran outside as the heavy drops of rain began splashing against his head and Kaliq threw his head back and shouted out her name.

'Eleni!'

But there was no sound from her. Nothing. His heart was pumping fit to burst, his stomach acid with fear. It was like being catapulted back to a time he had kept strictly off limits but he felt it again as if it were yesterday. The terror and dismay when he and his twin had discovered young Zafir missing. Those feelings of hopelessness and despair. The sensation of powerlessness—that he was too late to save the child from an unknown fate.

What if he was too late to save Eleni?

He could see the flash of something pale against the trees on the far side of the lawns. Was that her? Sheltering against the frightening prospect of attacking dogs—or sheltering from the harshness of her cruel and thoughtless lover?

Instinct took over as he dashed across the slippery grass with the increasingly heavy rains pelting down and soaking him to the skin. From within the murky depths of the heavy clouds he thought he caught the ominous rumble of thunder and his heart flared with a renewed fear. What if lightning struck the tree beneath which his lover was sheltering!

'Eleni!' The distraught word was torn from his lips as he ran towards the woods and now he could definitely see the pale shape of a figure. The barking was increasing and, although Kaliq had competed and won many races during his time in the Navy, never had he run as fast as he did just then. Instinct powered his body just as surely as it drew him towards her. And now he could see more clearly…because yes, *yes*—it *was* her! His frightened and soaking Eleni huddled beneath a tree—her eyes huge with disbelief as he ran towards her.

He reached her in seconds—gathering her into his arms just as the barking of the dogs reached a crescendo.

And then everything went crazy.

There were spotlights and searchlights as figures and animals circled them—the light picking out the gleaming teeth of highly trained guard-dogs as they strained against the leashes of the powerful men who restrained them.

Eleni thought that she saw the barrel of a gun pointing at her but her shaking fears were quelled—if only temporarily—by the protective warmth of Kaliq as he pulled her close into his body and wrapped his arms around her and started yelling.

'Stop!' His imperious command rang out and at the same moment someone must have recognised just who it was who spoke for the dogs were silenced as if by magic, and the most senior of the bodyguards stepped forwards and bowed deeply.

'Highness—'

But Kaliq cut him short with an impatient and furious interrogation. Were the dogs and the guards so stupid not to have realised that they were threatening his *guest*?

Eleni listened to the bodyguard's stumbled explanation, which was again cut short by a furious dismissal, and as the sodden and dispirited men and dogs crept away she actually felt a little sorry for them. Until she realised that maybe it was easier to feel sorry for total strangers than to feel sorry for herself. Or have to face the awful reality. The real reason why she had come running out here in the first place—as if that would help her escape the terrible inevitability of her situation. She stared at the ground, determined that Kaliq would not feel burdened by her heartbreak as she prepared to thank him for saving her.

'And now…'Kaliq was undeterred by the drops of rain which were continuing to drip through the leaves. His mouth curved at the corners—for wasn't this like stepping back in time to when he had first met her? 'Look at me, Eleni.'

Eleni thought that his voice was oddly gentle, more gentle than she had ever heard him before—expect perhaps when he was speaking to a horse—and, slowly, she raised her eyes to his.

Kaliq sucked in a breath—because even in the darkness he could see the bright beauty which had first so entranced him. A prince ensnared by a stable girl. It should never have happened—but it had. Had the great, guiding hand of fate been at work? he wondered dazedly. Because somewhere along the way she had forced him to confront his deepest fears, and, in so doing, to defeat them. He had done all he could to save Zafir, he realised—and now he must move on and accept that. Live in the here and now and take what was staring at him so beautifully in the face.

He suddenly realised that he felt light. Lighter than he had done in years. A burden lifted from his heart and his mind and all because of this one woman—his loyal and true, his feisty and determined Eleni.

He had planned to tell her that she should never have run away. Never have put herself in danger like that—but those words did not come. Others did. Strange, unfamiliar words which he felt as if he had waited all his life to say.

'I love you, Eleni,' he said simply. 'And I want you to be my bride.'

It was perhaps auspicious that the moon chose just that moment to appear from behind the fast-scudding clouds—which meant that Eleni could see from the shining clarity in her prince's eyes that he meant everything he said. But even if it had been pitch-black she would have believed him. Because Kaliq Al'Farisi was reckless, yes, but never with words.

Her heart was beating faster than when she had fled from the sound of the barking dogs and she lifted her hands to cup his dear, sweet face, swallowing down her tears of joy and offering him her tremulous smile.

'I love you, too, my darling. My darling, darling Kaliq,' she whispered as his face came down to blot out the pain of the past.

EPILOGUE

THE world's media went crazy.

THE PLAYBOY SHEIKH AND THE STABLE GIRL, screamed the tabloids. The international broadsheets commended the Sheikh Kaliq for his very modern attitude in taking such a low-born bride—and applauded the refreshing fact that a member of such a noble royal family should be marrying for love instead of power.

There were photos of the couple every-where. Eleni and Kaliq snapped leaving a res-taurant in London. Images of them boarding a jet in Madrid—and later on a trip to Paris. There were shots of them at the racecourse—and lots taken on Eleni's first visit to America when she took that country by storm. And finally the official photographs, which were issued by the Calistan palace on the occasion of their marriage. And what a marriage it was.

Nobody who was there would ever forget the sight of Nabat the horse—his neck garlanded with bright flowers—as he carried the bride through the teeming streets to the ceremony.

World leaders and members of every royal house flocked into the country guaranteeing a star-studded guest list—which put Calista high on the list of most-wanted destinations. But there were plenty of other guests, too— Amina was there, and so was Zahra, as well as Kaliq's huge, extended family. Even some of the Aristo royal family were represented at what was being called the wedding of the year, and to Kaliq's amazement Eleni had insisted on inviting her father.

'After everything he did to you?' he demanded.

But Eleni had laid a loving hand on the cheek of her proud sheikh. 'I must forgive him, my darling,' she said softly. 'For without forgiveness we cannot properly move on.'

And since Kaliq had finally learnt to forgive himself, he had caught that hand and kissed it, for he had known that what she said was true. But then, she always spoke the truth, his darling Eleni. It had been her advice which had led to him starting up an international charity for missing children which was being funded by his Calistan polo club. It might never bring Zafir back, but, hopefully, there were others it would.

Eleni's wedding band was made of the very finest Calistan diamonds—and her golden veil, which shimmered to the ground like a stream of sunlight, was crowned by an even more glittering circlet of the precious gems. Bright diamonds indeed.

But all the guests agreed that the brightest things on display were the eyes and the smiles of Prince Kaliq Al'Farisi and his new Princess Eleni.

millsandboon.co.uk Community

Join Us!

The Community is the perfect place to meet and chat to kindred spirits who love books and reading as much as you do, but it's also the place to:

- Get the inside scoop from authors about their latest books
- Learn how to write a romance book with advice from our editors
- Help us to continue publishing the best in women's fiction
- Share your thoughts on the books we publish
- Befriend other users

Forums: Interact with each other as well as authors, editors and a whole host of other users worldwide.

Blogs: Every registered community member has their own blog to tell the world what they're up to and what's on their mind.

Book Challenge: We're aiming to read 5,000 books and have joined forces with The Reading Agency in our inaugural Book Challenge.

Profile Page: Showcase yourself and keep a record of your recent community activity.

Social Networking: We've added buttons at the end of every post to share via digg, Facebook, Google, Yahoo, technorati and de.licio.us.

www.millsandboon.co.uk